The Bell in the Fog

A Collection of Supernatural Tales of Love, Death, and the Afterlife

A Modern Translation

Adapted for the Contemporary Reader

Gertrude Atherton

Translated by Tim Zengerink

Table of Contents

Preface - Message to the Reader

What If You Could Help Rebuild the Greatest Library in Human History?

Thousands of years ago, the Library of Alexandria stood as the crown jewel of human achievement — a sanctuary where the collected wisdom of every known civilization was gathered, preserved, and shared freely.

And then, it was lost.

Through fire, conquest, and the slow erosion of time, humanity lost not just books — but ideas, dreams, discoveries, and stories that could have changed the world forever.

Today, the Library of Alexandria lives again — and you are invited to be a part of its restoration.

Our mission is simple yet profound:

To rebuild the greatest library the world has ever known, and to translate all timeless works into every language and dialect, so that no seeker of knowledge is ever left behind again.

By joining our movement to rebuild the modern Library of Alexandria, you become part of an unprecedented mission:

- **Unlimited Access to the Greatest Audiobooks & eBooks Ever Written:**

  Instantly explore thousands of legendary works—Plato, Shakespeare, Jane Austen, Leo Tolstoy, and countless more. All instantly available to read or listen, placing a complete literary universe at your fingertips.

- **Beautiful Paperback & Deluxe Editions at Printing Cost**

  Own any title as an elegant paperback, deluxe hardcover, or stunning collectible boxset—offered to you at true printing cost, delivered straight to your door. Build your personal Library of Alexandria, crafted for beauty, built for durability, and worthy of proud display.

- **Fresh Translations for Modern Readers—in Every Language & Dialect**

  Enjoy timeless masterpieces reimagined in clear, contemporary language—no more outdated phrases or obscure references. Alongside the original versions, we're tirelessly translating these classics into every language and dialect imaginable, ensuring accessibility and understanding across cultures and generations.

- **Join a Global Renaissance of Literature & Knowledge**

  You directly support expanding our library, publishing deluxe editions at true cost, translating works into all global languages, and bringing humanity's greatest stories to people everywhere. By joining today, you're not just preserving a legacy of masterpieces; you set in motion a powerful wave of literary accessibility.

Become a Torchbearer of Knowledge.

Join us for free now at **LibraryofAlexandria.com**

Together, we will ensure that the light of human wisdom never fades again.

With gratitude and a shared love of knowledge,

The Modern Library of Alexandria Team

Visit:

www.libraryofalexandria.com

Or scan the code below:

Introduction

Art, Memory, and the Ghosts
That Speak Through Beauty

Gertrude Atherton's The Bell in the Fog, first published in 1905 as part of her collection The Bell in the Fog and Other Stories, stands as one of the most sophisticated and emotionally resonant ghost stories of early 20th-century American literature. Far from the traditional gothic haunted-house narrative filled with creaking staircases and howling phantoms, Atherton's story instead weaves a haunting of a different kind—one centered on memory, art, longing, and the ache of unfulfilled destiny. It is a story where the supernatural is not something to be feared, but something to be mourned.

Set in the tranquil yet brooding English countryside, The Bell in the Fog follows the American writer Ralph Orth, who rents the historic property of Chillingsworth in search of quiet and inspiration. The house, once the seat of an aristocratic family now faded into near obscurity, is filled with portraits, relics, and echoes of its past grandeur. It is in these remnants that Orth becomes enraptured—not by fear, but by fascination. He is particularly drawn to a painting of a young boy, known as "The Beautiful Child," a figure of ethereal beauty and sorrow who becomes a fixation for the writer. As the days pass and the fog thickens, Orth's artistic sensibilities and emotional instincts awaken something deeper—something that suggests the boy may not be a relic at all, but a presence still lingering, just beyond the veil of the real.

Atherton's tale unfolds not with screams or shocks, but with whispers. She uses atmosphere and suggestion to create a sense of ghostliness that is more spiritual than spectral. What haunts this story is not terror, but longing—the longing for beauty, for innocence, for the chance to restore what has been lost. The result is a ghost story of rare tenderness and melancholy, one that speaks less of vengeance or fear than of fragile connections between the living and the dead.

In this introduction, we will explore The Bell in the Fog through three major lenses: its use of gothic atmosphere and subtle symbolism, its psychological and emotional depth through the lens of aesthetic obsession and grief, and its broader significance in the evolution of supernatural fiction as a literary form of emotional and philosophical inquiry. We will also consider Gertrude Atherton's contributions to literature as a writer who challenged conventions and offered an American voice to the gothic tradition.

The Bell in the Fog is not merely a ghost story. It is a portrait of human vulnerability, captured in tones of grey and gold, framed by fog, and echoed by a bell no one else seems to hear.

The Haunted Mind:
Fog, Portraiture, and the Gothic Reimagined

From the very first lines of The Bell in the Fog, Atherton immerses the reader in a world where the past lingers just beneath the surface of the present. The landscape is classic gothic: a secluded estate with a shadowed history, shrouded in mists that obscure and reveal. But unlike the gothic fiction of the 19th century—where ruins, crypts, and storms serve as metaphors for overt terror—Atherton's use of setting serves as a metaphor for psychological liminality. Fog, here, is not only weather—it is memory, uncertainty, and the fragile line between perception and reality.

The house of Chillingsworth is filled with the signs of a once-great family, now faded. Yet it is not decaying in the traditional gothic sense—it is preserved. Portraits hang with undiminished grandeur. A chapel still stands. And it is in these details that Orth finds his own sense of wonder, not dread. The shift Atherton introduces is critical: instead of setting the reader up for fear, she prepares them for enchantment.

The key symbol in this story is the painting of the child—a boy of angelic beauty and tragic eyes, described in such tender and reverent detail that he seems to pulse with life. The portrait, like the bell in the title, becomes a focal point of ambiguity. Is it merely a painting? Or is it a spiritual vessel? Orth's relationship to the child begins with aesthetic admiration, but soon evolves into something deeper—an aching sense of connection, protectiveness, and identification. He begins to sense the presence of the boy throughout the house, in the air, in the silences between thoughts. Whether this is supernatural or psychological is never confirmed—and it doesn't need to be. The haunting is emotional, not literal.

Even the titular bell—once used in the family's private chapel, now long silent—becomes a symbol of resonance beyond hearing. Orth hears it once, faintly, like a call from another time. But no one else does. It is a sound meant only for him, a sign that he has tuned himself to a frequency others ignore. It marks the story's emotional turning point: Orth is no longer a tenant. He is now part of the house's memory, and it of his.

This redefinition of gothic elements—the substitution of ghost for emotional imprint, horror for melancholy, decay for beauty—marks The Bell in the Fog as a turning point in the genre. It shows that the gothic need not terrify to haunt. It can also ache.

Beauty, Loss, and the Artist's Desire

Ralph Orth, the story's central figure, is no gothic hero in the traditional sense. He is neither embattled nor paranoid, neither morally flawed nor especially courageous. Instead, he is thoughtful, sensitive, and above all, responsive—responsive to art, to feeling, and to history. He is, in essence, a vessel for aesthetic and emotional experience.

What drives Orth is not fear, but fascination. His attraction to the boy in the portrait is not simply artistic—it is emotional, even spiritual. The child represents a kind of beauty and innocence that Orth feels the world has lost, or perhaps that he himself never possessed. This sense of incompleteness, of yearning for something just out of reach, defines his emotional arc.

Atherton never makes this obsession grotesque or inappropriate. It is handled with restraint and deep sensitivity. The narrator does not seek possession of the child's image. He seeks understanding, even communion. In this way, the story becomes an exploration of the artist's heart—the ache to protect beauty, to honor it, to somehow preserve the sacredness of the past through art.

This emotional core is what makes The Bell in the Fog such a powerful ghost story. It is not about being scared. It is about being moved. The ghost here is not a wraith or poltergeist. It is a feeling, a presence, a longing that wraps itself around the soul like fog on a chapel steeple. The moment Orth hears the bell—perhaps real, perhaps imagined—is not a signal of danger. It is a signal of recognition. Something within him has awakened. Something remembered him back.

The tragedy of the tale lies in its final ambiguity. Orth leaves Chillingsworth with the sense that the child has either returned to sleep or crossed into peace. He has not saved the child, but he has witnessed him. And perhaps that was enough. Perhaps art, when met with true understanding, can set even the quietest ghosts free.

Gertrude Atherton and the Feminine Gothic Reclaimed

Gertrude Atherton (1857–1948) was a pioneering American novelist, essayist, and social critic who carved her place in a male-dominated literary world with bold, unapologetic works that spanned genres and defied convention. Though often remembered for her historical novels and feminist essays, Atherton's supernatural fiction deserves equal acclaim. In stories like The Bell in the Fog, she demonstrates a subtle and modern command of gothic form—one that aligns more with psychological insight and emotional depth than with sensationalism.

What sets Atherton apart is her rejection of formula. Her ghost stories are not vehicles for moral punishment or plot-driven horror. They are meditations on the unseen forces that shape identity, memory, and emotion. In The Bell in the Fog, she uses a male protagonist, but the story itself speaks with a feminine sensibility: intuitive, compassionate, melancholic, and quietly transformative.

Atherton also challenges the masculine conception of ghost stories as fear-based. Instead, she offers ghost stories that are feeling-based. Her specters do not scream. They gaze. They linger. They make you remember. And in that remembrance, they ask you to feel—not terror, but recognition.

In this, she paved the way for 20th- and 21st-century writers who would carry the gothic into the terrain of emotional realism. Writers like Shirley Jackson, Toni Morrison, and Sarah Waters all trace part of their lineage to the space that Atherton helped open—where ghost stories do not merely frighten but illuminate the human soul.

The Bell in the Fog is not a loud story. It is a quiet masterpiece. A story of stillness, beauty, and the moments in life when something ancient brushes past us, leaving a trace we cannot quite explain.

But we remember it. Just as Orth remembers the boy. Just as the bell, though silent, still rings.

And if you listen closely—through the fog—you may hear it too.

The Bell in the Fog

I

The famous author had finally achieved one of his biggest dreams from his younger years: owning an old family estate in England. It wasn't because he deeply cared about having ancestors or an old family name. What he really loved was the beauty, history, and quiet pride of ancient homes — places where generations of people had lived and passed on. He didn't care much about wealth by itself; he respected it only when it was earned by a smart and modern mind like his own. Seeing huge, expensive rooms decorated in one day with a pile of money made him uncomfortable, no matter how tasteful they looked. It even made him a little angry to see the old treasures of Europe shipped over to decorate shiny new American houses. It felt wrong to him, and even went against the sense of patriotism he kept tucked away inside. In his opinion, if the average American wasn't an artist at heart, they had no reason to pretend to be world travelers. They were American through and through — from the way they talked to how restless they were — and their homes should reflect that.

Orth had left the United States not long after his first big successes. His work was so great it couldn't be tied to one place anymore, and people had stopped calling him an American author. He used the whole of Europe as a stage for his stories. Even though his writing wasn't colorful or full of wild passion, it was incredibly original and powerful. His clever ideas didn't always get noticed — and often didn't — but the beautiful, mysterious way he wrote, and the deep intelligence behind it, won over those who truly understood him.

His fanbase wasn't large, but it was made up of the most important and respected people. In fact, if you didn't admire Ralph Orth, you were basically admitting you didn't belong among the best. Of course, truly elite groups are small, and many of their members borrowed books from libraries instead of buying them. On the European continent, people picked up cheaper editions. If Orth hadn't inherited enough family money to keep an apartment on Jermyn Street and dress like a wealthy English gentleman, he might have had to write more popular stories just to survive. Luckily, he didn't have to worry about that. The fashionable and high-society circles of London not only knew who he was, but wanted him around. He was smart enough not to let himself become a passing trend, and polished enough never to annoy or bore people. Because of that, his popularity stayed steady year after year, and he was eventually seen as one of their own.

He wasn't crazy about sports, but he could handle a gun well enough, and men respected his calm, noble presence. Women cared more about his books than men did, maybe because most men didn't have the patience for his style. (Here, we're talking about men-of-the-world — the seasoned, worldly types.) A group of young writers — and a few women — practically worshipped him. They copied his style, and Orth, who had a hidden soft side beneath his formal manners, appreciated the attention. Eventually, he wrote fancy "reviews" about all of them — essays that hardly anyone could understand, but which still worked just fine because his name was attached.

Despite all this success, Orth wasn't fully happy. Every year, from August through winter — unless he decided to go to Homburg or the Riviera — he stayed at England's finest country houses, sleeping in grand guest rooms and walking through historic parks. But what he really wanted, deep down, was his own piece of land to call home.

He was almost fifty when his great-aunt passed away and left him her fortune. In her will, she wrote that it was "a small reward for his lasting contributions to literature." The inheritance was a big one. Suddenly, there was a rush to buy his books, and new editions were quickly announced. He smiled, a little bitterly and sadly at the same time, but he was truly grateful for the money. As soon as he found a place that met his high standards, he bought an estate in the countryside.

The new home was everything he had ever dreamed of — he had spent years imagining owning a place like this, even more than he had ever dreamed about love. The land had once belonged to the Church, and the ruins of an old cloister and chapel stood sharply outlined against the pale sky above the ancient woods. Even the main house was from the Tudor period, carefully maintained over generations by wealthy owners. The lawns were smooth like velvet, the hedges were perfectly trimmed, and the trees were old and full of history, just like the settings he created in his stories. It wasn't a grand castle or a huge estate, but it was perfect in its own way. For a long time, he felt like a man on an endless honeymoon. He would often pause to run his hand gently along the rough, ivy-covered walls.

After settling in, he started inviting friends to visit. His invitations, offered with a certain careful pride, were never turned down. Americans traveling through England often tried to get introduced to him. Even though they sometimes felt awkward around his cold, formal manner — and the quietness of Chillingsworth — they were thrilled just to meet him. They hoped for clever conversations, and many rushed out to buy complete sets of his books afterward. Still, they were usually too nervous to ask him for an autograph.

Although women often called him "brilliant," a few men who knew him better said he was actually gentle and kind. Some of them were happy to spend weeks with him at Chillingsworth, even with no one else around. Still, overall, Orth lived a pretty lonely life.

He realized just how lonely he was one bright morning in June. Sunlight poured through the tall, narrow windows, lighting up the tapestries, old armor, and family portraits left behind by the former owners. The golden light dusted the dark wood of the walls and floors. At that moment, Orth was standing in the long gallery, studying one of his favorite paintings — a portrait of a young boy dressed like Robin Hood. The boy looked confident and full of life, with a face so beautiful that it touched Orth deeply, no matter the boy's personality.

But today, as Orth stared at the boy's shining face, something stirred inside him beyond just admiration for the painting.

"I wish he were alive and here with me," Orth thought with a deep sigh. "He would make a wonderful little companion. This grand old house would suit him far better than it suits me."

He turned away quickly, only to find himself standing before another portrait — this time of a little girl. She was very different from the boy, but just as perfect in her own way. It was obvious that the same artist had painted both, and Orth had always believed they must have been brother and sister.

The girl was angelically beautiful, with fair skin so light it almost seemed see-through. Her dark blue eyes were deep and thoughtful, even though she looked no older than six. Her small mouth, shaped like a delicate scarlet curve, stood out against her pale face. Her soft, pale hair fell in gentle waves over her bare shoulders — not the stiff curls most children wore back then. She wore a simple white dress and clutched a fancy doll dressed in far richer clothes than her own. Behind her, the ruins and woods of Chillingsworth stretched into the distance.

Orth had admired the painting many times before, mostly for the artist's incredible skill. But today, all he saw was the child herself. The boy's portrait faded from his mind as he became completely drawn into the beauty and spirit of the little girl.

"I wonder if she lived long enough to grow up," he thought. "With those eyes and that face, she could have become an amazing, even famous, woman. But could a spirit as pure as hers really survive the harsh truths of adulthood? Maybe a mind like hers — one that had been cleaned of life's usual flaws — would have hated the ordinary struggles of a woman's life. Maybe it's better when perfect beings stay perfect by leaving the world early. Still, it's possible that the artist who painted her made her look more perfect than she really was — maybe he painted his dream of the perfect child."

He turned away from the painting, feeling restless. "I guess I'm actually pretty fond of children," he admitted to himself. "I catch myself watching them on the street when they're especially cute. Well, who doesn't like kids?" he added defensively.

He tried to get back to work. He was writing a story meant to be the main feature of a new magazine. After about half an hour, he tossed down his pen — a "wondrous instrument" that really just looked like a regular pen — and gave in to the urge to go back to the gallery. The only faces he could focus on were the proud little boy and the angelic little girl. It was like they were calling out to him from across time, and deep inside, something old and faint stirred in response.

"It's the dead recognizing the dead," he thought. "But I wish these children were alive."

For the next week, he kept wandering into the gallery, and the children's faces stayed in his mind. Then he started to feel annoyed at himself.

"I'm acting like a childless woman longing for kids," he said out loud. "I need to do something to get these children out of my head."

With the help of his secretary, he searched through the house's library and finally found the gallery catalog listed in the inventory. That's where he discovered their names: the boy was Viscount Tancred, and the girl was Lady Blanche Mortlake, the son and daughter of the second Earl of Teignmouth. Still not satisfied, he sat down and immediately wrote a letter to the current Earl, asking if he knew anything about the children's lives.

He waited for the reply with a level of impatience he wasn't used to, taking long walks and purposely avoiding the gallery.

"I think these kids have completely taken over my thoughts," he admitted to himself. "They are beautiful, though. The last time I looked at them, especially in the soft evening light, they almost seemed alive. I wish they were alive — running around this park."

Lord Teignmouth, who admired him greatly, wrote back quickly.

"I'm afraid I don't know much about those ancestors — the ones who didn't do anything big," the Earl said. "But I do remember my unmarried aunt — she keeps up with all the family history — once telling me that the little boy drowned in the river. The little girl died young too — she just kind of wasted away, I think. I'm terrible at writing letters, and honestly, I wouldn't even dare write to you if you weren't such a great man. Anyway, that's all I know. I'm pretty sure the artist who painted them knew more about them than anyone else."

When Orth read the letter, he felt strangely relieved that the girl had died young, though he was sad for the boy. Even though he had stayed away from the gallery lately, he had imagined a whole brilliant future for the young Viscount — a bold, exciting life full of achievements. Sometimes he even wished he could have helped guide such a strong spirit. He caught himself feeling jealous of the old dust of the past that had been closer to the boy than he ever could be.

When he learned the boy had died young, even though he regretted the loss of so much potential, part of him was secretly glad. At least now, the boy belonged to no one else. Smiling to himself with a mix of sadness and humor, he thought,

"What an old fool I am. I don't just wish those kids were alive — I wish they were mine."

That honest admission was his undoing. He went straight back to the gallery. After some time apart, the boy's portrait seemed even more full of life, and the little girl's soft smile almost begged to be picked up and hugged.

"I need to try something else," he thought desperately after spending a long time staring at them. "I have to write them out of my system."

He returned to the library and locked away the serious story he had been working on, which no longer held his interest. Instead, he began to write about the short lives of the two children, surprising even himself because he usually didn't write such simple stories. But before he finished three chapters, he realized he was creating a masterpiece — and more than that, he was feeling a happiness so intense that sometimes his hands shook and his eyes blurred with tears.

His characters had always been distant, admired mostly for their beauty and cleverness, not for feeling alive. He had always been fine with that. His real satisfaction had come from crafting beautiful sentences and shaping his characters like delicate statues. But the boy and girl were different. He had loved them in his heart long before he ever thought of putting them into a story, and the moment he began writing, they seemed to leap off the page, full of life.

The old house echoed with their laughter and playful mischief. Orth didn't really know much about children, so the adventures he invented for them were fresh and original. The little girl clung to him, following the boy on their wild adventures. Realizing how real they had become to him, Orth imagined them filling every room of the mansion, so that each corner would carry memories he could hold onto after they were gone.

He even chose their bedrooms and imagined staying up with them through not childhood illnesses, which were beyond his experience, but the small accidents and adventures that come from being young and brave. He forgot all about the real second Lord Teignmouth; in his mind, he was the children's father, and he admired himself for it — something art alone had never made him do. Strangely, in his imagination, the children had no mother — not even the memory of one.

He wrote the book more slowly than usual, taking great joy in thinking about what the next chapter would hold. But as he neared the end, he started to feel a kind of fear. He decided that once he finished the book, he would leave immediately for Homburg. Every day, he visited the gallery because he no longer wanted to erase the children from his heart. Now they truly belonged to him.

Sometimes he had to remind himself — almost jokingly — that they had been born to someone else, and that their real bones rested under the old chapel. But even knowing that, he refused to visit the family tombs where their marble statues lay. In lighter moods, he would even laugh at how lucky he was that his great-aunt's fortune had helped him "buy" what little was left of them.

For two months, he lived in this dream world. But finally, he knew the story had to end. He forced himself to write about the little girl falling ill. When he wrote the scene of holding her small hands as she faded away, his own hands shook and his legs trembled. The whole house felt empty and broken without her. He wished he had left one part of it untouched by memories, somewhere he could hide from the sadness.

He stayed away from his writing desk for two days, avoiding the river in the park as if it frightened him. When he finally returned to work, he made an important decision: the boy would live. He couldn't bear to kill them both. The boy's death in real life had been an accident, and Orth felt it was fair to let him survive — with a hint of future greatness to come. But even letting him go off into the world at the end of the story felt painful, like losing a real son.

When the book was finished, he packed his bags immediately. He sent the manuscript to his publisher without even rereading it, asked his secretary to check it carefully, and left the next morning for Homburg.

In Homburg and around Europe, he quickly forgot about the children. He visited many grand houses and kept himself busy until November, when he returned to London. To his surprise, he found that his book had become the talk of the literary world. His secretary gave him the reviews, and for once, Orth actually read what critics said.

He found himself celebrated as a true genius, compared even more favorably to the brilliant talent people had known as Ralph Orth for twenty years. It pleased him — every writer wants to be called a genius, and he was no exception. Some writers are lucky and praised right away; others, like him, had to wait. Orth had waited a long time — long enough to see many "geniuses" forgotten — and now it was finally his turn.

Still, he knew deep down that no amount of praise could match the happiness he had felt while writing that book. It was the brightest joy he had ever known, and for a man who had written many books by the age of fifty, that was saying something.

He let London's social scene celebrate him for a month, then cancelled all his plans and returned to Chillingsworth.

His estate was in Hertfordshire, a place of gentle hills, twisting country roads, ancient oak trees, wild open fields, and old houses steeped in history — a peaceful, timeless corner of England. As Orth's carriage drove through his gates, he saw a perfect English sunset — a streak of red sky with a church spire silhouetted against it. His woods were still and quiet. Even the cows in the fields seemed to understand the calm beauty of the moment. The ivy on his gray stone towers had once been young when his imagined children were alive.

That night, he hardly slept, haunted by memories. But the next day, something even stranger began to happen.

II

He woke up early and went for one of his long walks. England always seemed to invite people to walk its land, and Orth, like many others who had moved there, felt the strong urge to wander while enjoying a peaceful mind. But today, as on other recent days, he couldn't find that peace. His thoughts were as restless as his feet.

After two hours of walking, he wandered into the woods of a neighbor's estate — a place he usually avoided. It had been bought by an American widow who loved hunting, and Orth didn't care much for her loud, flashy ways. Just then, he heard children's voices and quickly turned to leave.

As he turned, he suddenly came face-to-face with a little girl standing on the narrow path. For a moment, he was overwhelmed by a horrible feeling — pure terror. It felt like his body and soul were falling apart. The child standing in front of him looked exactly like the little girl from the portrait he loved so much, only more alive and beautiful. Even in his panic, he noticed she seemed even more real and full of spirit than the painting had shown.

Luckily, the fear only lasted a second. The little girl spoke.

"You look really sick," she said. "Want me to help you get home?"

Her voice was soft and sweet, but her accent was clearly American — and not a very refined one. In a way, the shock of hearing her speak was even worse than seeing her face. But this time, Orth pulled himself together.

"Who are you?" he asked sharply. "What's your name? Where do you live?"

The little girl smiled, a kind, sweet smile, though she seemed a little amused.

"I've never had someone ask me so many questions at once," she said, smiling. "But that's okay. I'm just happy you're not actually sick. I'm Blanche, Mrs. Jennie Root's daughter — my daddy passed away.

We live in Rome, New York. We're just here visiting some of my dad's family." Orth took her hand. It was warm and soft.

"Take me to your mother," he said in a serious voice. "Right away. You can come back and play afterward. And I promise — I'll send someone to town today to get you a beautiful new doll." At first the girl's face looked a little disappointed, but when she heard about the doll, she lit up with joy. Still, she walked beside him very seriously. Orth sighed inside when he realized she was leading him toward the widow's estate, but he made up his mind to find out everything he could about the child — even if it meant talking to the woman he disliked so much.

To his surprise, though, the girl didn't take him into the big house. Instead, she led him toward an old stone cottage that once belonged to the tenant farmers.

"My great-great-great-grandfather lived here," she said proudly, her American pride in her ancestors clear.

Orth didn't smile. If not for the feeling of the girl's small hand in his, and her sweet voice, he might have felt like he had stepped into one of his own ghost stories.

The girl led him into the dining room, where an old man was sitting at the table reading a Bible. The room looked ancient — probably at least 800 years old. A thick black tree trunk held up the ceiling, and the small windows still had their original leaded glass. Through a doorway, he could see a large kitchen where several women were working.

The old man, who looked like he might have built the house himself, glanced up and gave Orth a hard, unfriendly look. But when he saw the little girl, his expression softened. He stood up and offered Orth a chair. At the same time, the women from the kitchen came into the room.

"Of course you've fallen for Blanche," one of the women said, laughing. "Everyone does."

"Yes, that's it. Exactly," Orth said, still feeling a little dazed. He decided to be completely honest. "This little girl surprised me because she looks exactly like a portrait I have at Chillingsworth — a painting from about two hundred years ago. Things like this don't usually happen by accident. I admired that portrait so much that I even wrote a story about it. So you'll understand why I'm very curious to find out if there's a real connection. The little girl told me her ancestors lived here, and since my little girl's portrait lived next door, it makes sense that there could be a link."

The old man quietly closed the Bible, slipped his glasses into his pocket, and slowly left the room.

"He'll never talk about family secrets," said one of the women, who introduced herself as the old man's daughter. She placed some bread and milk in front of Orth. "Every family has its secrets, and we have ours too. But he won't ever tell those old stories. What I can tell you is that one of Blanche's ancestors got himself into trouble because of a rich lady. He ended up killing himself. His sons didn't turn out well either. One of the boys saw what happened and was never right afterward — he was simple-minded. The mother wasn't strong enough to guide the other boy, and there seemed to be a curse on the family for a long time. Things didn't start getting better until one of them went to America. Since then, well, they haven't exactly gotten rich, but they've managed, and at least they don't drink like they used to."

"They haven't done all that well," said another woman, who looked worn and tired. Orth guessed she belonged to the small-town middle class in the eastern United States.

"You're not the child's mother, are you?" he asked.

"Yes, sir. Everyone is surprised — you don't have to apologize," the woman said. "She doesn't look like any of us, even though her brothers and sisters are good enough for anyone to be proud of. We all think she must have wandered into the family by mistake because she looks like she could be a rich lady's child. And, well, we're just middle-class."

Orth was stunned. It was the first time he had ever heard an American describe themselves as middle-class. For a moment, he forgot all about the child. His sharp mind was already studying this new and unexpected discovery. He asked some questions and learned that the woman's husband had owned a hat store in Rome, New York. Her sons worked as clerks, and her daughters had jobs in shops or did typing work. Together, they supported her and little Blanche — who had been born long after her other children had grown up — and they were a very happy family. The boys sometimes got into trouble, but overall, they were good sons. The daughters, she said proudly, deserved much better opportunities than they had. All her children were strong and healthy — except for Blanche.

"She came along so late in my life, when I wasn't young anymore," she said, blushing slightly in that modest American way. "That's why she's delicate. But I think she'll be fine. She couldn't be taken care of better even if she were a queen's child."

Orth, who had gratefully finished the bread and milk she gave him, stood up.

"Is that really all you can tell me?" he asked.

"That's all," she answered. "And you'll never get a word out of my father about it."

Orth shook hands warmly with all of them. When he wanted to, he could be very charming. He offered to walk Blanche back to her friends in the woods, and she happily grabbed his hand.

As they were leaving, Orth suddenly turned back to Mrs. Root.

"Why did you name her Blanche?" he asked.

"Because she was so white and delicate — it just seemed to fit her."

Orth took the next train to London. There, he got Lord Teignmouth to give him the address of the aunt who knew all the family stories, along with a letter of introduction. After that, he spent an hour in a toy shop, picking out gifts — something he hadn't even thought of doing for the book-children he had once written about. He chose the best doll he could find, along with a tiny piano, a set of fancy toy dishes, a toy kitchen, and a little playhouse. He happily signed a check for thirty pounds, feeling a strange joy he hadn't expected. Then he caught a train to Lancashire, where Lady Mildred Mortlake lived in an old family estate.

Many writers, especially those with vivid imaginations, are drawn to the idea of the unseen and the mysterious. Creative people seem naturally closer to the forces that shape the universe, maybe even a small part of those forces themselves. So it's not strange that writers often feel a connection to things beyond the visible world — or at least enjoy the idea of it. Orth had always been open to such ideas. He didn't claim any strong personal beliefs, but his imagination had wandered into the unknown more than once and brought back ideas for his stories.

Lady Mildred welcomed Orth warmly, happy to meet the generous man who had helped keep their old family name alive. She listened eagerly to everything he had to tell — the things he hadn't shared with the world — and to the strange twist involving the American child.

"I'm completely lost," Orth said finally. "What connection did my little girl have to the tragedy? How was she related to the woman who caused that young man's death?"

"She was the woman," Lady Mildred said quickly.

Orth stared at her, feeling once again that strange sense of everything falling apart inside him. Lady Mildred, pleased by his reaction, continued more calmly:

"Wally was up here visiting right after I finished your book, and I realized he gave you the wrong story about the portrait. Not that it's his fault — we've kept the real story quiet as much as possible. I'm only telling you because, if I didn't, you'd probably obsess over it forever.

"Blanche Mortlake — your Blanche — didn't die as a child. She lived until she was twenty-four. She was a beautiful, angelic child, but little angels sometimes grow into very naughty adults. I think she was always delicate, which made her seem even more spiritual. Maybe she was spoiled and praised too much, until her real self got lost. Anyway, she became the biggest flirt of her time. She loved breaking hearts, even after she got married. She hated her husband and behaved recklessly. She never had any children.

"So far, it's not a very unusual story. But the worst part — the darkest stain on our family's history — is what happened next.

"One summer, she was staying at Chillingsworth, hiding from her husband, when she met a young man named Root. He was from the neighboring estate and was considered a perfect example of a strong, handsome man — the kind that made great soldiers back then. He was already married and had two young sons, but he spent more time with his friends than with his family.

"Some say Blanche and Root met in the woods; others say he visited her at the house. Either way, he fell completely in love with her — and she either loved him back or pretended to. Maybe she really did love him — it happens. But even though I'm not easily shocked, I have a hard time believing women can stoop so low.

"They became the scandal of the whole county. After a while, maybe because she got bored with him, or because his rough manners bothered her, or because she feared her husband's return, she broke it off and went back to London.

"Root followed her there and forced his way into her home. Some say she softened and forgave him but made him promise never to see her again. He went back home and took his own life. A few months later, she killed herself too. That's all I know."

"That's more than enough," Orth said quietly.

The next night, Orth sat on a train traveling across the dark, wild lands of Lancashire. Everywhere he looked, giant chimneys spit out flames into the sky. Where the sky wasn't glowing red, it was pitch black. The place looked like hell itself.

Normally, Orth's imagination would have been thrilled by such a scene. The quiet beauty of southern England had nothing to match the fierce, terrifying energy of these burning fields. The chimneys were hidden in the thick darkness, and the fires seemed to burst straight from the earth's core.

Orth was lost in his own thoughts, thinking about everything he had ever heard about the supernatural. He remembered the belief that when sinners die, they are forced to stay close to the world for a long time, trapped between life and death. Eventually, they must return to earth to fix the wrongs they caused, often among the families they hurt. He also remembered that people who believe in the occult see suicide as a terrible sin, something cursed and hated.

Writers, Orth thought, are closer to the hidden truths of the universe than most people because of their daring imaginations — the same imaginations that often annoy critics. Just like only those who risk mistakes achieve great things, only those who set their imaginations free sometimes catch glimpses of the mysteries beyond the ordinary world. If those writers make mistakes, it's not for ordinary people to judge them.

When Orth returned to Chillingsworth, he immediately went to visit Blanche and found her happily playing with all the gifts he had sent. She threw her arms around his neck and kissed his face. From that moment, Orth adored her completely, loving her simply for who she was, without thinking about the strange mystery anymore.

Soon he found ways to spend more and more time with her. They started with long walks, then lunches at his home. Before long, she was spending whole days at Chillingsworth. He even set up a nursery filled with toys and hired a nurse to watch over her. They went to London to see plays and to buy Christmas gifts for her family. Together, they decorated the biggest, most beautiful Christmas tree Chillingsworth had ever seen. She even had a donkey-cart to ride around in.

After a month, Blanche was living like a little princess at Chillingsworth and visiting her mother every day. Mrs. Root seemed proud and very pleased. Orth told her directly that he planned to take care of Blanche and make sure she had a good education. Since Mrs. Root planned to stay in England for six months, Orth decided not to tell her yet about his deeper plans for the child's future.

He began teaching Blanche better grammar and speech and read her books that would have confused most children her age. But she listened happily, even if she didn't always comment. He played games with her when she wanted, but she was gentle and tired easily. Most days she preferred curling up in a big chair, warming her toes by the fireplace, while Orth read to her or talked.

Although she liked to dream and often seemed deep in thought, Orth saw nothing strange or unnatural about her. She had a sharp sense of humor and laughed easily like any other child. Orth had almost given up hoping that anything mysterious would happen with Blanche. She seemed so full of warmth and love that everyone who met her, from the author himself to a litter of puppies from the stables, adored her.

One warm summer day, Orth decided to take her to the gallery. Until now, he hadn't dared — the gallery was too cold during winter and spring. Although part of him wanted to see how she would react to the old portrait, another part was afraid of what he might discover. Still, when sunlight streamed through the gallery windows, he led Blanche inside.

At first, they wandered around, looking at the other paintings. Orth pointed out different pictures and shared his thoughts, and Blanche smiled and listened politely. He never knew exactly how much she understood, but the mystery of her quiet depth fascinated him even more.

Finally, he turned to the portrait of the little girl — the one who had haunted him for so long. He hesitated, then pointed to it.

"What do you think of that?" he asked. "Remember, I told you how much you look like her."

Blanche glanced at the painting without much interest, but Orth noticed her skin suddenly turned from its usual pure white to a soft gray color.

"I've seen it before," she said. "One day I came in here by myself to look at it. And I've come back a few times since. You never told me not to," she added quickly, looking at him shyly before dropping her gaze. "I really like the little girl — and the boy — a lot."

"Why do you like them?" he asked.

"I don't know," she said — a phrase she often used when she didn't want to explain something. Her eyes stayed down, but she looked calm. Orth didn't press her. Instead, he just watched and waited.

After a moment, she shifted a little uncomfortably but didn't giggle or act nervous like most children would. Blanche was always calm, always full of life and affection. She seemed made for love, and everyone she met loved her back. Death, Orth thought, would never have made her more serene — she was already the picture of peace.

Finally, she lifted her eyes, but instead of looking at him, she looked at the painting.

"Did you know there's another picture hidden behind that one?" she asked.

"No," Orth said, feeling a chill run through him. "How do you know that?"

"One day, I touched a secret spring in the frame, and the painting moved. I can show you if you want."

"Yes," he said. Part of him was curious, and part of him hated the idea of a hidden spring, like something cheap in a story.

Blanche touched the frame, and the portrait of the little girl swung aside so quickly it looked like someone had shoved it. Orth narrowed his eyes and stared at what was revealed, forcing his face to stay calm even though he was breathing hard.

Behind the first painting was a portrait of the same Blanche Mortlake, but now fully grown into a beautiful woman. There was no doubt it was the same person — the spiritual look from her childhood was mostly gone, except maybe in the sadness around her mouth. In her place stood a strong, brilliant young woman, full of restless energy. Even the way she wore her pearl necklace showed a kind of pride. Her whole presence seemed rebellious, alive, and almost dangerous.

Orth turned quickly to Blanche, who was now studying the new portrait.

"What a tragedy that is!" he said, trying to sound cheerful. "Think about it — a woman like that, born two hundred years ago, stuck in a boring family, probably married off to some dull man. No wonder she caused trouble. If she had lived today, she would have used her talents and become famous — and she wouldn't have wasted her life chasing silly romances."

He bent down and lifted Blanche's chin so she would look at him, but she didn't meet his gaze.

"You look exactly like that little girl," he said softly, "but you're even purer and finer. She never had a real chance. You will. You live in a time where women can become anything they want. I'll make sure you have every opportunity. Whatever you want to be, you will be. No bottled-up dreams or wasted talents for you. We'll teach you to be strong, and you'll grow into a woman who knows how to use her freedom."

She slowly lifted her eyes and gave him a long, heartbreaking look full of sadness. Her chest rose once in a deep breath, then she pressed her lips tightly together and looked down.

"What do you mean?" he burst out, his voice rough because he was so shaken. "Is it — do you — ?" He couldn't bring himself to finish the thought. Finally, he said awkwardly, "You mean you're afraid your mother won't let me adopt you when she leaves? That you guessed what I want? Tell me, will you?"

But Blanche just lowered her head and turned away. Afraid of upsetting her more, he apologized for speaking so harshly, carefully slid the original painting back into place, and led her out of the gallery.

He sent her up to the nursery, and when she came down for lunch and sat beside him, she acted as cheerful and innocent as always. For a few days, Orth held back his questions. But one evening, as they sat together by the fire listening to a storm outside — just after he finished telling her a story about the erl-king — he lifted her onto his knee and gently asked what she had been thinking about that day in the gallery when he had imagined her bright future.

Once again, her face lost its color, turning a soft gray, and she looked down.

"I can't say," she whispered. "Maybe... I don't know."

"Was it what I guessed?" he asked.

She shook her head, then looked at him with such a scared, pleading look that he dropped the subject immediately.

The next day, Orth went alone to the gallery and stared at the portrait of the grown woman. She stirred nothing inside him. Nor could he imagine the woman Blanche might grow into ever feeling anything romantic toward him. What he felt for Blanche was purely a father's love, and it would never change.

He went outside and found Blanche digging happily in her little garden, dirt smudging her clothes and face. The next afternoon, sneaking into the hall quietly, he caught her sitting in her big chair, staring into space, her face full of sadness. When he asked if she felt sick, she quickly smiled and said she was just tired.

After that, Orth noticed she spent more and more time curled up in her chair and rarely played outside unless he was with her. She kept insisting she was fine, but several times he caught her with a look so sad that it broke his heart. Worried, he called in a famous children's doctor from London.

The doctor examined her carefully. After Blanche left the room, he shrugged and said,

"She might have only ten years in her, or she might live a full, strong life. I honestly can't tell. She looks healthy on the surface, but I don't have X-ray vision. She might be perfectly fine — or quietly fading. She has the look of children who don't live long. I've never seen a child more spiritual-looking. But there's no clear sign of illness. Keep her outdoors, don't spoil her with candy, and make sure she doesn't catch anything."

That summer, Orth and Blanche spent almost every day outside, either under the trees in the park or riding through the quiet country lanes. He didn't invite guests, and he didn't write. Every part of his heart belonged to Blanche. She was his constant joy, and he didn't care about the rest of the world.

Blanche's health didn't seem to get worse, and Orth's fears slowly faded. He even convinced Mrs. Root to stay in England for another year. Orth sent her tickets to plays every week and gave her a horse and carriage to enjoy herself. She seemed happy, spending less and less time with Blanche.

He took Blanche on trips — two weeks at Bournemouth, and another trip to Scotland — both of which she loved. She had become a little queen in his life, bossing him around playfully. But she was always sweet, honest, and filled with that deep mystery Orth could never quite explain. She adored him and didn't seem to want any other company, though she was always loving toward her mother when they met.

It was during the tenth month of this peaceful time that Mrs. Root burst into the library at Chillingsworth, where Orth happened to be alone.

"Oh, sir," she cried, flustered, "I have to go home! My daughter Grace wrote to me — she should have told me sooner — the boys aren't behaving right. She didn't want to worry me while I was having such a good time, bless her, but now I have to go. I just can't stay. Boys are such a responsibility — girls aren't nearly as much trouble, even if mine can be a handful."

Orth, who had written about enough women to know when to stay silent, let her talk until she ran out of breath. Then he spoke calmly:

"I'm sorry this has come so suddenly, because it forces me to bring up something I hoped to mention slowly over time."

"I know what you're going to say, sir," she interrupted quickly. "I've been feeling guilty that I didn't warn you earlier. You want Blanche — I could see that — but I can't let her go, sir. I just can't."

"Yes," Orth said firmly, "I want to adopt Blanche. And honestly, I don't think you should say no. You know it would be the best thing for her. She's a remarkable child. She deserves every opportunity — not just money, but the right surroundings. If I adopt her legally, she'll become my heir. She could grow up to be as great a lady as any in England."

Mrs. Root turned pale and began to cry.

"I've spent so many nights lying awake, fighting with myself," she said when she could finally speak. "I've already given her up a little by letting her stay with you. I know I shouldn't stand in her way now — but she's dearer to me than all my other children put together."

"Then stay here in England," Orth said kindly. "At least for a few more years. I'll support you — you won't have to rely on your other children. You can see Blanche as often as you like."

"I can't do that, sir," she said, shaking her head. "I have six other children. I can't abandon them. They all still need me — even if it's just to hold them together. Three of my girls are still unmarried, and my boys can be wild. I can't leave them."

She hesitated, struggling with what to say next.

"There's something else, sir... I'm not sure how to put it," she said.

"Go on," Orth said gently.

In her eyes, he could see how much she admired him — the perfect gentleman in her mind — even though some of the other visitors at the estate thought him cold and proud.

"You have to understand," the woman said, "her brothers and sisters adore Blanche. They used to save every little bit of money they had just to buy her anything she wanted. I'm not sure what could make her happy now, but she's not spoiled at all. To them, she's almost like a religion, since none of us are really churchgoers.

"I'll tell you something I've never said to anyone — not even the kind family we're staying with. There's a bit of wildness in all my kids, but I believe Blanche is the one who keeps them steady.

"My daughters get frustrated sometimes — they work all week, don't have much fun, and don't meet the kind of men they dream of marrying. Sometimes they get so upset they say terrible things. But afterward, they always calm down and promise they'll live their lives for Blanche. They've said it over and over, and they mean it. Every sacrifice they've made for her has made them better people.

"Blanche isn't preachy. She never tries to lecture them or calm them down when they're angry. It's just her presence — who she is. Sometimes she'll just stand tall and give them a proud look, and it crushes them inside. They want her to respect them more than anything.

"I've become a little superstitious about her. Before she came along, I used to feel scared all the time. I believe she was sent to us because we needed her. So you see, I know she deserves more than we can give. She's too special for us. But her brothers and sisters deserve some thought too. They have good hearts — more good than bad.

"I just don't know what the right thing is. I've lost many nights of sleep worrying about it."

Orth stood up quickly. "Maybe you should give it more thought," he said. "You can stay a few more weeks. There's no need to rush."

The woman stood too. "I've made up my mind," she said. "Let's let Blanche decide. I believe she'll know what's right. I won't say anything to her or try to sway her. And I trust you won't either. She'll know."

"Why would you think that?" Orth asked sharply. "She's just a child — not even seven. You can't put that kind of decision on her."

"She's not like other children," the woman said calmly.

"I wouldn't know," Orth admitted. "I've never raised a child."

"I have," she said. "Six of them. And I've seen hundreds of others. I'm not the type to brag about my own, but Blanche... she's different. I'm sure of it."

"What do you believe?" Orth asked.

She said simply, "I think she's an angel who came to us because we needed her."

"And I think she's Blanche Mortlake, finishing her journey to find peace," Orth thought silently. But he didn't say a word and soon found himself alone.

Several days passed before Orth brought it up with Blanche. One morning, while she was sitting on the grass with the sun shining on her, he told her gently that her mother would soon have to leave.

To his shock — and secret happiness — Blanche burst into tears and threw herself into his arms.

"You don't have to leave," he said softly once he found his voice. "You can stay here forever and be my little girl. It's your choice."

"I can't stay," she sobbed. "I can't!"

"Is that why you've been so sad lately?" he asked, desperate to understand.

She said nothing.

"Oh, Blanche," he whispered, full of emotion. "Trust me. Tell me what's in your heart. You're the only living thing I love."

"If I could explain, I would," she said through her tears. "But I don't really know — not completely."

"Then what do you know?" he asked gently.

But she just cried harder and stayed silent. Orth knew he couldn't push her any more. After all, she was still just a little girl, even if her spirit seemed older.

"All right," he said. "Let's talk about something else. Your mother says your brothers and sisters might suffer if you leave. Do you think you really make that much of a difference to them?"

"Yes," Blanche whispered.

"How do you know that?"

"Do you know how sometimes you just know things?" she said softly.

"No, but I trust your instincts," Orth said. "Still, your brothers and sisters are grown enough to live their lives without leaning on a child. Soon they'll be married and starting their own families. Your mother will have grandchildren to keep her company.

"But me — if you leave — I'll be all alone. I won't say I'll fall apart, but I'll be the loneliest man in the world."

Blanche pressed even closer to him, her small hands clutching his coat tightly.

"Can't you come too?" she asked in a small voice.

"No, my dear," he said gently. "You would have to live completely with me or not at all. Your world and mine are too different. We wouldn't fit together. And if you lived with me across the ocean, you'd still be just as far from your family.

"If they really love you, your memory will inspire them even if you're not there."

"Not unless I die," she said quietly.

Something inside Orth froze. "Do you think you're going to die young?" he asked, almost afraid to hear the answer.

But Blanche said nothing.

The next day, Orth walked into the nursery and found her packing up her dolls. When she saw him, she sat down and began to cry helplessly.

He knew then that he had lost her.

And a year later, when he received her last little letter, he was almost grateful she had left the world when she did.

The Striding Place

Weigall, always a little distant and detached, got bored quickly with grouse hunting. Standing behind a sod wall while workers drove the birds toward the shooters made him feel like a weak copy of the ancestors who once roamed these moors and forests in real hunts. But every August he still accepted invitations out of habit, and in return, he would invite his hosts to shoot pheasants at his estate in the South. He believed you had to accept the pleasures of life with the same attitude as you accepted its troubles.

That day had been a bad one. Heavy rain had made the moor so soft that the ground seemed to bounce underfoot. The grouse seemed to have disappeared, and the hunters had little to show for their work. The women at the castle were no better — most were dull, except for a bold young debutante who had annoyed Weigall at dinner by asking him to describe the faded paintings on the ceiling above them.

But none of these things were really weighing on Weigall's mind as he slipped out of the castle after the others went to bed and wandered down toward the river. What troubled him was that his closest friend — the companion of his boyhood, his college roommate, and his travel partner — had mysteriously disappeared two days ago. It was as if he had vanished into thin air.

His friend, Wyatt Gifford, had been staying at the neighboring estate, spending his days happily shooting grouse and flirting with Adeline Cavan. He had seemed in the best of spirits. There was no reason to think he was depressed: he was wealthy, Miss Cavan clearly liked him, and he was one of the best shots in England — nothing seemed wrong. No one believed he had taken his own life, and there was no sign he had been murdered. But two nights ago, he had left March Abbey without a hat or coat and had not been seen since.

Search parties had been out nonstop, with workers combing the woods and poking through the moors, but no sign of him had been found — not even a handkerchief.

Weigall didn't believe for a second that Gifford was dead. Although the situation was worrying, he was more angry than scared. At Cambridge, Gifford had been a notorious prankster and loved pulling off wild stunts. It would be just like him to sneak off into the night dressed in evening clothes, hop onto a train full of cattle, and enjoy the chaos he had left behind.

Still, Weigall cared too much about his friend to sleep peacefully, so instead of going to bed, he decided to walk until he was too tired to think. He made his way down to the river, following a path through the woods. There was no moon, but the stars gave a cold, faint light over the river as it wound past trees, rocky cliffs, and ruined walls. The river gurgled over stones, scolding sharply where it had to, then calmed again when the way was clear.

The deeper Weigall walked into the woods, the darker it became. He smiled, remembering something Gifford had once said:

"An English wood looks wonderful from far away, but up close it's just a disappointment. You can see daylight on both sides, and sunlight even freckles the ferns. Our forests need the night to seem as deep and mysterious as they should be — like they were before our ancestors' descendants started demanding more money and comfort."

Weigall kept strolling, smoking as he walked, thinking about his friend and remembering the many conversations and jokes they had shared. Just a few months earlier, at the end of the London season, they had spent an entire night walking the streets after a party, talking about what happens to the soul after death.

That afternoon, they had attended the funeral of a college friend who had spent his last three years lost in madness. They had visited him once in the asylum and found his face old and ruined by illness. But when they saw him dead, his face looked young again, almost like the friend they had once known.

They hadn't had time to talk about it then, but that night, walking the streets, they returned to the topic.

"I like to believe," Gifford had said, "that sometimes the soul lingers in the body after death. When someone is insane, the soul is trapped — helpless but aware. Imagine the horror of that. So when the body finally dies, maybe the soul stays a little longer, reclaiming the body one last time before moving on. It's a chance for the soul to say goodbye properly, to be honored as it should be. If it were me, I'd stay with my body until it was safely buried with my ancestors. Then maybe I'd feel ready to move on. Otherwise, my curiosity might drag me off into the unknown too fast."

"You believe the soul and the body are separate things, then?" Weigall had asked.

"Absolutely," Gifford had said. "They're like twins — sometimes friends, sometimes enemies — but they're loyal to each other in the end. Someday, when I get tired of life, I'll go to India and become a mahatma, just to see proof of that bond."

"What if you couldn't get back into your body after one of your 'astral trips'?" Weigall had joked. "Wouldn't that be a mess?"

Gifford had only laughed. "Maybe. But it would be an interesting problem to solve."

Suddenly, the loud roar of rushing water broke into Weigall's thoughts. He had reached the Strid — a narrow, dangerous part of the River Wharfe where the water squeezed between massive rocks, boiling furiously as it passed through. The woods rose dark and silent on either side, and above him, the stars seemed colder and sharper.

The river on either side of the Strid seemed to disappear into endless blackness. There was no lonelier spot in England — and if ghosts existed anywhere, it would be here.

Weigall wasn't a coward, but he shivered remembering all the grim stories about this place. Wordsworth's famous Boy of Egremond had supposedly died here, and many others had tried to jump the Strid and never been seen again. People believed that under the surface was a natural cave where bodies got trapped forever.

Weigall stood on the rocks, imagining the bones hidden below, picked clean by eyeless creatures. Then he wondered if anyone had tried to jump across recently. The stones were slick with slime — more dangerous than he had ever seen them.

"This crossing is called the 'Strid,'" the old rhyme said. "It's had that name for a thousand years, and it will keep it for a thousand more."

Weigall shivered and turned to leave, feeling a sudden need to get far away from the place. But just as he moved, something caught his eye — something white moving in the foamy water below the waterfall. It didn't move with the water; it fought against it, rising and pulling backward.

Weigall froze, barely breathing. It felt like his hair was standing on end. Was that a hand? It lifted higher above the churning water, turned sideways, and he clearly saw four fingers clawing at the air in front of the black rock.

His fear disappeared at once. A man was trapped there, fighting for his life, caught in the river's strong pull. He must have fallen in just minutes ago — maybe even while Weigall had been standing nearby.

Carefully, Weigall moved closer to the edge. The hand was shaking wildly, as if cursing the river's strength, then it opened wide again, reaching out for help.

Weigall ran to the nearest tree, tore off a branch with all his strength, and raced back to the river. The hand was still there, waving desperately. Whoever it was had gotten stuck in the rocks below, maybe jammed halfway into one of those hidden underwater shelves.

Weigall climbed down onto a lower rock, braced his body against it, leaned out over the rushing water, and shoved the branch toward the hand. The fingers clutched it immediately.

He pulled with everything he had, but at first, nothing happened. His feet slipped dangerously close to the edge. Then, all of a sudden, an arm broke free above the water.

His heart pounded so hard he could barely see. For a moment, he felt like the river was pulling him in too. But he forced himself to focus.

Now he could see the sleeve — and the cufflinks. They had a special design he recognized instantly.

It was Gifford.

Weigall forgot the danger, forgot everything except saving his friend. He pulled harder than he ever had in his life, even as his muscles screamed in pain. Memories rushed through his mind — all their college days, their crazy adventures, their long talks that had lasted until morning.

He had loved women before, but nothing compared to the bond he had with Gifford. In all his thirty-two years, he had never trusted or cared about another man so deeply.

Weigall threw himself flat on the rocks, holding on desperately. His wrists ached, his hands were bleeding, but the fingers still gripped the branch.

Suddenly something gave way. The hand spun around, and the branch was ripped from his grasp. The body broke free from the rocks and was swept downstream.

Weigall scrambled to his feet and raced along the rocks, knowing the worst was over now. The river would carry Gifford to the calm pool ahead. And Gifford, who was so strong in the water, had a chance — if he survived the beating of the current.

When Weigall reached the pool, he saw a man floating on the surface, still wearing his evening clothes. One arm had hooked over a rock, holding him in place. His hand hung down, white and still, above the dark water.

Without thinking, Weigall splashed into the shallow pool, grabbed Gifford, and pulled him to the bank. He yanked off his own coat to move more freely, ready to try everything he knew to save him.

For a moment, he hesitated. Was there still a chance? He hadn't looked at Gifford's face yet or checked for a heartbeat. But he couldn't waste time.

He turned toward his friend — and froze.

Something hit him — something horribly wrong. At first, he couldn't even understand what he was seeing. His teeth clashed together, and his arms shot out in shock.

But he forced himself to kneel down and look.

There was no face.

The Dead and the Countess

(Republished from the Smart Set)

The cemetery was old, and the people buried there had been dead for a long time. These days, anyone who died was buried in a new graveyard up on the hill, closer to the Bois d'Amour and near enough to hear the church bells calling people to mass. But the small church that still held services stood beside the older graves. No new church had been built in that forgotten corner of Finisterre for hundreds of years — not since the stone cross had been raised in the village square, surrounded then, as it still was, by simple gray cottages. Not since the castle with its round tower had been built down by the river for the Counts of Croisac.

Even though it was old, the stone walls around the cemetery were well cared for. There were no weeds and no broken headstones. It looked cold, gray, and lonely, like most cemeteries in Brittany, but it wasn't messy or run-down. It was quiet and respectful.

Sometimes, it even looked beautiful. Every year during the village's pardon — a religious festival — a big parade left the church. Priests wore bright, shiny robes. Young men in black and silver costumes carried tall, sparkling banners. Girls in white headpieces and black dresses decorated with lace and ribbons marched past the graves, singing. They honored the generations before them — villagers who once carried those same banners and sang those same songs.

Most of the people buried there had been peasants and priests. The noble family, the Croisacs, had their own private cemetery hidden in the hills behind the castle. In this little graveyard rested old men and women who had once wept for fishermen lost at sea, and even a few children.

Whenever people passed the cemetery — during a festival, after a wedding, or any church event — they always looked serious and sad. The women grew up knowing life would be filled with fear, waiting, and loss. The men knew the sea could give life or take it away. Life was hard, and death often came as a blessing. The living didn't envy the dead, and the dead didn't envy the living either. They only pitied the women washing clothes by the river, looking beautiful but carrying hard burdens.

The dead lay quietly in their graves, grateful to finally rest in peace.

But even their peace would not last forever.

The village was beautiful and unique — even for Finisterre. Artists found it and made it famous. After the artists came the tourists, and soon the old creaky carriages were replaced by something new. Brittany became a trendy place to visit for a few months each year, and where fashion goes, a railroad usually follows.

The new railway built for the crowds ran right past the little cemetery.

At first, the dead didn't notice. They didn't hear the workers hammering or the first blast of the train's whistle. They didn't know that the old priest had begged for the tracks to be placed somewhere else.

One night, the priest sat on a grave and wept. He loved his dead, and it broke his heart to think that the greed of businessmen and the fast pace of modern life would shatter the sacred peace of those who had already suffered enough. He had known many of them in life, because he was very old himself. And even though he believed in heaven, purgatory, and hell like all good Catholics, in his heart he pictured his friends sleeping quietly in their coffins — their souls and bodies resting together — patiently waiting for the final call.

He wasn't a scholar or a dreamer, just a simple priest with a strong imagination. He liked to think the dead still lay whole and undisturbed, not as broken bodies abandoned by their souls. And in his mind, all who sleep eventually wake.

He knew the dead had slept through terrible storms that wrecked ships on the rocky shores and tore down trees in the Bois d'Amour. They had not stirred during the soft chanting of pardon processions or the sound of bagpipes at village weddings. All those things they had once known in life — but they no longer heard or cared.

But the train was different. It was loud and violent enough to shake the earth and tear apart the silence. It wasn't like a storm or a celebration. It was a noise so harsh that neither the living nor the dead could ignore it.

The priest would have given anything to protect his dead. But the railway was built anyway. And the first night the train screamed past, shaking the church windows and rumbling the ground, the priest went out and sprinkled holy water on every grave.

From that night on, every morning and every evening, whenever the train rushed by, he went out with his holy water — whether he was sick or whether the weather was terrible. He believed it helped — that the dead were locked even deeper in their sleep.

But one night, something changed.

It was late, and the sky was almost black, with only a few stars shining. No wind came from the plains or the sea. It was a peaceful night — no storms, no wrecks. The village was silent and dark, except for a single light burning in the tower of Croisac castle, where the young countess was gravely ill.

The priest had been sitting with her when the train roared past. As the sound faded, she had whispered to him:

"I wish I were on that train. This place is so lonely — this cold, echoing castle where I see no one day after day. If it kills me, mon père, please promise you'll bury me by the road where I can hear the train passing, the train that goes to Paris. If they put me over the hill, I'll scream in my coffin every night."

The priest had done what he could to comfort the soul of the young noblewoman, someone far different from the people he usually helped, and hurried back toward the old cemetery. As he walked along the dark road, his stiff legs aching, he thought about how strange it was that she had the same wish he did.

"If she truly meant what she said, poor young thing," he murmured aloud, "then I won't sprinkle holy water on her grave. Those who suffer in life should have what they want after death. And I fear the count doesn't care for her the way he should." He tucked his robe under his arm and began to pray quietly as he hurried along.

But when he reached the cemetery and went among the graves with his holy water, he heard something — a faint muttering coming from below.

"Jean-Marie," a voice said, shaky and rough, as if struggling to find the right sound, "are you ready? Surely that must be the final call."

"No, no," rumbled another voice, deep and steady. "That's not the sound of a trumpet, François. It will be sudden and sharp, like the great winds that roar down from the icy gorges of Iceland. Do you remember those winds, François? Thank God they let us live long enough to die in our beds, with our grandchildren beside us and just a soft breeze blowing through the Bois d'Amour. Ah, the poor friends we lost — those who went out one too many times to the grande pêche and never came back. Do you remember when that huge wave wrapped around Ignace like his wife's arms? We never saw him again. We thought we'd be next, but we lived and went to sea again and again, until we finally died peacefully at home. Thanks be to God!"

"Why are you thinking about that now—here in the grave, where none of it matters anymore?"

"I don't know. But as I lay dying, that was the last memory I had — that night Ignace was taken. What were you thinking of when you died?"

"I was thinking about the money I owed Dominique. I wanted to ask my son to repay it, but death came too fast, and I couldn't speak. God knows how they remember me now in St. Hilaire."

"You're forgotten," said another voice, quietly. "I died forty years after you. People don't remember for long in Finisterre. But your son was my friend, and I remember that he paid your debt."

"And what about my son? Is he here too?"

"No," the voice answered. "He's deep at the bottom of the northern sea. It was only his second trip, but he came back the first time with a purse full of money for his young wife. After the second voyage, he never returned. She washed clothes for the ladies of Croisac to survive, but she didn't live long after. I wanted to marry her, but she said losing one husband was enough. I married someone else. Every three years I spent at the grande pêche aged me ten."

"Did you come here an old man?"

"I was sixty. My wife died before me, like many wives do. She's buried here too. Jeanne!"

"Is that you, my husband?" a woman's voice answered, faint and trembling. "Is it really you? I thought that terrible noise was the trumpet calling us to judgment."

"It couldn't be, old Jeanne," he said. "When the trumpet sounds, we'll have wings and robes of light and fly up to heaven. Have you been sleeping well?"

"Yes. But why are we awake now? Is it time for purgatory? Or have we already been there?"

"Only God knows. I remember nothing. Are you scared? I wish I could hold your hand, like when you slipped away from life and into this long sleep you feared but also welcomed."

"I am scared," she whispered. "But it's sweet to hear your voice again, even if it sounds hollow and strange from the grave. Thank God you buried me with my rosary." She began praying quickly, telling the beads.

"If God is good," cried François harshly — and the priest clearly heard his voice, as if the coffin lid had rotted away — "then why have we been woken too soon? What devil was it that thundered through my mind like that? Has God been defeated and the Devil taken his place?"

"Stop!" said another voice. "You must not blaspheme! God rules now and always. This must be some punishment for our sins on earth."

"We were punished enough when we were alive," said François. "Why should we suffer even after death? It's dark and cold here. Will we lie like this forever? We wished for death when we lived, but now...

I would rather be alive again, even poor, old, and in pain. Anything would be better than this. Curse the monster that woke us!"

"Don't curse, my son," said a softer voice — and the priest, hearing it, stood up, removed his hat, and crossed himself, because he recognized it as the voice of the priest who had come before him.

"I don't know what this is," the old voice said, sad and weary. "Something has shaken us in our graves and torn our spirits out of their blessed sleep. I don't like being aware of this narrow coffin, or feeling the heavy earth pressing down on my heart. But it must be right — it has to be right — otherwise it wouldn't be happening. Ah, me!"

A baby's soft, hopeless crying floated up from underground. From another grave nearby, a mother's voice rose, trying desperately to calm her child.

"Oh, dear God!" she cried. "I thought the final call had come— that I would rise, find my baby, and be with my Ignace again, my Ignace whose bones lie white at the bottom of the sea. Father, when the dead rise, will he find them? Lying here not knowing—that's worse than being alive."

"Yes, yes," the priest answered gently. "Everything will be alright, my daughter."

"But it's not alright, Father," she said. "My baby is crying alone, trapped in a little box underground. If only I could dig my way through the dirt to her—but my old mother's grave lies between us."

"Pray!" the priest ordered firmly. "Say your beads. If you don't have a rosary, say the 'Hail Mary' one hundred times."

At once, a low, steady muttering filled the cemetery as the dead whispered their prayers. Everyone obeyed—except the baby, whose soft, broken crying continued. Knowing they would stay quiet the rest of the night, the priest went into the church to pray until sunrise. His heart was heavy—not for himself, but for the restless dead.

When the sky turned pink and the air smelled fresh with morning, a piercing scream shattered the silence. The priest hurried outside and sprinkled double the usual amount of holy water on the graves. The train raced by, letting out two sharp, mocking whistles. Before the ground had even finished shaking, the priest pressed his ear to the earth.

Sadly, they were still awake.

"The demon is flying past again," said Jean-Marie. "But when he passed, I felt as if God's finger touched my forehead. It can't hurt us."

"I felt it too!" said the old priest. "And I!" "And I!" "And I!" came from every grave—except the baby's.

Relieved that his prayers had brought them some comfort, the priest hurried toward the castle, forgetting he hadn't eaten or slept. He wanted to make one final appeal to the count, who was a railroad director.

It was early, but no one in Croisac was sleeping. The young countess had died. A high-ranking bishop had arrived during the night to give her the last rites. Hoping for help, the priest asked if he could speak with the bishop. After a long wait in the kitchen, he was finally allowed upstairs.

He followed a servant up the wide spiral staircase. On the twenty-eighth step, he entered a room draped with purple cloth stamped with golden fleurs-de-lis. The bishop lay high above the floor in one of the old grand beds built into the walls of Brittany's homes. Heavy curtains shaded his cold, pale face. The small, bent priest felt even smaller and struggled to find the right words.

"What is it, my son?" the bishop asked in a cold, tired voice. "Is it truly urgent? I am exhausted."

Nervously, stumbling over his words, the priest tried to explain the terrible unrest among the dead. But as he spoke, he realized how crazy he must sound. Even though he knew the truth in his heart, it felt hopeless to explain.

The bishop, who had been looking around the room distractedly, suddenly locked eyes with him—and burst into fury.

"And this is your emergency, you babbling fool?" he roared. "You wake me up with a bunch of nonsense—as if I were just another crazy old man like you! You're not fit to be a priest or to care for souls! Tomorrow—"

But the priest had already run out, hands wringing in despair.

As he stumbled down the staircase, he ran straight into the count. Monsieur de Croisac had just closed a door behind him but opened it again and silently led the priest inside.

There, high up against the wall, the young countess lay at rest, her hands forever clasped in prayer. Pale flames flickered at the head and foot of her grand carved bed. The blue curtains and old rugs in the room were faded, showing just how far the Croisac family's fortunes had fallen since the days of the Bourbons.

The count lived in the crumbling château because he had no other choice. Tonight, he bitterly regretted bringing a young girl into such loneliness. Maybe, he thought, there were things he could have done to save her from sadness—and death.

"Pray for her," he told the priest. "And bury her in the old cemetery. It was her last wish."

He left, and the priest dropped to his knees to pray. But as he mumbled, his eyes kept drifting to the tall, narrow windows. He imagined how the countess must have spent hours staring out at the fishermen heading north, followed by their worried wives and mothers. Sometimes there would be nothing to see but the dark river, the woods, the ruins, or the rain stabbing into the water.

Weakened by hunger and exhaustion, the priest let his mind wander. He wondered if the young woman's soul was finally free, away from the restless mind and worn-out body. From where he knelt, he couldn't see her face—only her waxy hands clutching the crucifix. He wondered if death had smoothed her features or if she still looked sad and angry, as she had in life.

Curiosity pushed him forward. He cut his prayers short, pulled a chair to the bed, climbed up, and leaned close to look.

Sadly, her face was not at peace. It was full of bitterness and sadness. Even in death, her nose was tense, and her lip curled slightly, as if her last words had been angry ones. Yet, even thin and worn, she was still very beautiful. Her long black hair spilled over the bed, and her heavy lashes cast shadows on her sunken cheeks.

"Poor little one," thought the priest. "No, she won't find peace. She wouldn't even want it. I won't sprinkle holy water on her grave. If that awful train brings her any comfort, let it."

He went into the small oratory next to the bedroom and prayed even harder. But when the watchers came an hour later, they found him collapsed in a faint at the foot of the altar.

When he finally woke up, he was lying in his own bed beside the church. Four days passed before he could move about again—and by then, the young countess had already been laid to rest.

The old housekeeper left the priest alone to take care of himself. He waited eagerly for nightfall. A steady, soft rain was falling—a gray, quiet rain that blurred the landscape and soaked the ground of the Bois d'Amour. The cemetery was wet too, but the priest barely noticed. After all, he had spent a lifetime ignoring his own discomforts.

When he heard the distant whistle of the evening train, he hurried outside with his holy water. He sprinkled every grave except one just as the train roared past.

Then he knelt and pressed his ear to the ground, listening carefully. It had been five days since he last came here. Maybe, he hoped, the dead had finally fallen back into their deep sleep.

But within moments, he was wringing his hands and crying to heaven. The ground beneath him was full of sorrowful voices. They cried out for mercy, for peace, for rest. They cursed the evil force that had broken the locks of death. Among the many voices—of men, women, and children—the priest recognized the trembling prayer of the old priest who had come before him, not cursing but pleading bitterly.

The baby screamed with pure terror, and the mother's voice rose frantically, too desperate to comfort her child.

"Ah," cried Jean-Marie's voice, "if only they had told us what purgatory was really like! What do the priests know? They warned us about punishment, but no one said it would be like this. To sleep for a few hours, only to wake up to another horror! To hear the earth itself insult us! And then the terrible noise of hell, again and again! Oh God! How long must this go on?"

The priest staggered to his feet and rushed across graves and muddy paths to the mound where the young countess was buried.

Maybe, he thought, her voice would be different—maybe she would praise the rushing train and be grateful for the sounds that had shattered the others' peace.

He knelt and put his ear to her grave. At first, he heard nothing. Pressing harder against the wet ground, he held his breath and listened. A deep, rumbling moan rose up from below, then another, and another. But there were no words.

"Is she crying with sympathy for the others?" the priest wondered. "Or have they frightened her? Why doesn't she speak to them? Maybe if she told them about the world they left behind, it would comfort them. But it was never really their world. Maybe that's what makes her sad. Maybe she's even lonelier now than she was alive."

Suddenly, a sharp, horrified cry pierced the ground. It was followed by a gasping shriek, then another—all fading into a dreadful, muffled rumble.

The priest stood up and looked desperately toward the rainy sky.

"Alas!" he sobbed. "She is not at peace. She made a terrible mistake. She wanted the sweet deep rest of death, but instead, the monster of iron and fire—and the restless dead around her—are torturing her poor soul. Maybe there's peace for her in the vault behind the castle, but not here. I know what I must do. I must act now."

He gathered his robes and ran as fast as his aching legs and swollen feet could carry him toward the castle, whose lights shone faintly through the rain.

Near the riverbank, he met a fisherman and begged for help. Without question, the fisherman lifted the priest into his boat and rowed quickly to the château. When they reached the other side, he tied up the boat.

"I'll wait for you in the kitchen, Father," said the fisherman. The priest blessed him and hurried inside.

Once again, he entered the huge kitchen, with its blue tiles and shining brass pans, relics from the days when kings and nobles visited Croisac in its glory. He collapsed into a chair near the stove, shivering. A maid quickly ran to find the count.

She returned and said, "My master will see you in the library."

The library was a gloomy room. It smelled of old leather from the ancient books lining the shelves. A few new novels and newspapers were scattered on the heavy table. A fire burned weakly in the fireplace. The wallpaper was dark and the gold fleurs-de-lis were faded and dull. The count sat waiting, looking tired and grim.

When at home, the count usually split his time between this room, the river, and hunting in the forests. But he often escaped to Paris, living like a bachelor in one wing of his grand hotel. He had loved his young wife once, but her sadness and endless longing for the lively world she had once known had pushed him away. Over the past year, he had stayed distant, resentful and cold.

Now, too late, he understood. Now he was overwhelmed with guilt and regret. She had been full of spirit, intelligence, and hunger for life. And he had given her so little in return.

He realized, bitterly, that bringing her here—into a lonely, crumbling château—had been a terrible mistake.

The count stood up as the priest entered and gave him a deep bow. The visit annoyed him, but he still respected the old priest, who had performed many important ceremonies for the family over the years. The count moved a chair toward him, but the priest shook his head and twisted his hands nervously.

"Forgive me, monsieur le comte," the priest said, "maybe you too will call me an old fool, like the bishop did. But I must speak, even if you order your servants to throw me out."

The count flinched slightly. He remembered the bishop's harsh words and the suggestion that a younger priest should replace the old one, who they thought was no longer fit for duty. Still, he replied politely:

"You know, my father, no one in this house would ever disrespect you. Say whatever you need to say. But please, sit down. I am very tired."

The priest finally sat and looked at the count with pleading eyes.

"It's this, monsieur," he said quickly, afraid he might lose his nerve. "The terrible train—with its iron body, burning coals, filthy smoke, and screaming whistle—has awakened my dead. I protected them with holy water, and for a long time they slept peacefully. But one night, I was away with madame when the train went by, shaking the earth and loosening the nails in the coffins. I hurried back, but it was too late. The dead had awakened. Their deep, eternal sleep was broken. At first, they thought it was the Last Judgment, but when they realized it wasn't, they tried to comfort each other. But now they are desperate. They are trapped in a nightmare, monsieur, and I have come to beg you to help move them far up the hill—where they can finally rest."

He stopped, breathing hard. The count listened without changing his expression, certain he was dealing with madness. He was growing impatient, and his hand drifted toward the bell on the table to summon help.

"Ah, monsieur, not yet!" cried the priest, gasping. "It's about the countess too. I almost forgot. She wanted to be buried near the road, to hear the trains going to Paris, so I didn't sprinkle her grave with holy water. But she is not at peace either! She moans and cries out. Her coffin is strong and new, so I can't hear her words clearly, but I heard her tonight, monsieur—I swear it on the cross! Ah, now you believe me!"

The count had gone pale as death and was shaking all over. He staggered out of his chair, staring at the priest as if he had seen a ghost.

"You heard—?" he gasped.

"She is not resting, monsieur. She moans and screams from her grave, as if someone's hand is covering her mouth—"

The priest never finished his sentence. The count suddenly turned and ran from the room. The priest wiped his forehead and slowly sank to the floor.

"He will believe me now," he thought as he drifted into sleep. "Tomorrow he will help my poor friends."

Now, the old priest lies high on the hill, far away from the noise of any train. His friends from the disturbed cemetery are buried close beside him. The Count and Countess of Croisac, who grew to honor his memory, made sure to give him in death the peace he had longed for in his final days. And with them, too, all things are well—for sometimes, even the living can be born again without having to pass through the grave.

The Greatest Good of the Greatest Number

Norton Blaine came back to New York after a short vacation and found a desperate letter waiting for him. It was from John Schuyler, the person he cared about most, besides himself. The note begged him to "come at once" and, like always, hinted that the favor would be for God's sake, not just a man's.

The letter was already a day old. Without even changing his clothes, Blaine called for a cab and sped uptown. He wasn't the emotional type—he was a man of science, cold, sharp, and brilliant, like a perfect machine that kept getting better. But for this one friend, he always made an exception. They had been close since they were boys, and their respect for each other's talents had only deepened over time.

As the cab rolled down the Avenue, Blaine casually glanced at the carriages returning from the Park, tipping his hat to a few of the fashionable women inside. His small fame came from being able to handle the delicate nerves of high society. He could calm a hysterical woman with just a firm hand or a sharp tone. Some even said his eyes could smoke with anger.

Suddenly, he leaned forward and tipped his hat more thoughtfully. A woman in one of the carriages acknowledged him. She was pale and striking, with strong features and deep, intense eyes—the kind of woman who could shake the world if life ever knocked her off course. She lounged back in her seat, chatting with a faded older woman. But when her eyes met Blaine's, her mouth tensed for a moment. They shared a quick, knowing glance before she raised her chin boldly, almost daring him—or anyone else—to judge her.

Moments later, Blaine arrived at Schuyler's home. Schuyler was pacing back and forth in the library, looking terrible—his hair was messy, his clothes were wrinkled, and he hadn't shaved. His handsome face, full of strength and hidden weakness, lit up with relief when Blaine walked in.

"She's been awful," Schuyler said right away. "I didn't have the heart to call anyone else, and now I'm completely worn out. She's sleeping now, and I finally escaped for a half-hour. Even the nurse is exhausted. Please, stay tonight."

"I'll stay," Blaine agreed. "Let's go up."

As they climbed to the second floor, two young children rushed across the hall and threw themselves into their father's arms.

"Where have you been?" they asked. "Why do you stay upstairs with Mama all the time? When is she going to get better?"

Schuyler kissed them and gently sent them back to the nursery.

"How long can I keep hiding it from them?" he said bitterly. "What a terrible home for my children to grow up in."

"If you'd take my advice and send her where she belongs—" Blaine started to say.

"I won't," Schuyler cut him off sharply. "She's my wife. If we sent her away, it would be impossible to keep it secret."

They reached the third floor. Schuyler slid a key into the lock but paused for a moment.

"I saw in the paper that she was back," he said suddenly. "Is it true?"

"I saw her on the Avenue a little while ago," Blaine answered.

For a brief second, he thought he saw a desperate look in Schuyler's eyes.

They entered a room where the doors and windows were covered to block sound. The furniture was heavy and solid, nothing easy to move or break. There were no mirrors anywhere.

Lying on the bed was a woman. Her hair was tangled, her skin yellow and hollow, but somehow, she still had an air of faded elegance. Her dry, blistered lips were cracked and dark, and her thin hands gripped the blanket like the claws of a bird of prey. A strong but exhausted nurse sat beside her.

The woman opened her eyes. They had once been called beautiful, but now they looked like dark stains on paper.

"Give me a drink," she rasped. "Water! Water! Water!" She panted, her tongue slipping out slightly. Schuyler turned away, trembling. The nurse quickly lifted a silver cup to her lips, and she drank hungrily.

Then she looked up at Blaine with a scowl.

"You missed it," she said bitterly. "I should be glad, because I hate you—but you're better than the rest. They're cowards. They tried to trick me—the fools! But they didn't try it again. I bit them."

She laughed and threw her arms above her head. The loose sleeves of her gown slid back, showing her arms, which were covered in small dark spots like burns.

"Just another morphine addict," the doctor thought coldly. "And she's John Schuyler's wife!"

About an hour after dinner, Blaine told Schuyler and the nurse to get some sleep. He stayed alone with the woman, reading while she slept deeply. The house was completely silent—or at least it seemed that way. Even if there had been noise, this part of the house was so isolated, he probably wouldn't have heard it. The window was open, but it only looked out over rooftops and backyards. No sounds of carriages or people reached him.

Even with the quiet, Blaine had to listen closely to catch the woman's uneven breathing.

He had a strange feeling—odd for a man who never let his imagination get in the way. It felt like this third floor had been sliced away from the rest of the house and now floated alone in space, cut off from everything. The thought grew stronger once he lost interest in his book, an idea that had been quietly creeping through his mind.

Finally, he closed the book and walked over to the bed, looking down at the woman with cold, detached eyes—like a scientist studying a wounded animal.

One look at Blaine's face showed he wasn't someone easily shaken by emotions. His skin was pale as marble. His profile was sharp and perfect, his mouth a thin, hard line. His chin was square and strong, his deep gray eyes cold and sharp as polished steel. His broad forehead seemed to glow, a sign of the powerful mind inside.

As he studied the woman, his thin nostrils twitched once, and his mouth tightened even more. Then, suddenly, he smiled—a strange, almost wicked smile.

"A doctor," he said half out loud, "has almost as much power as God. Maybe that's what we really are."

He stuffed his hands into his pockets and began pacing the thickly carpeted room.

"Here's the truth," he thought. "The one man I truly respect is trapped—tied down by that broken creature on the bed. She's beyond help. Every cure has failed—and will always fail—because she loves the drug too much. Meanwhile, he's brilliant—one of the best minds of our time—and a man full of heart and loyalty. And yet, at forty-two, he's forced to live with daily humiliation and fear.

"And now, after all these years, he meets a woman who captures his heart and his imagination—someone who finally matches the dream he's carried. She makes him forget every other woman. But he can't marry her. That woman on the bed could live another twenty years."

He stopped pacing, clenching his fists.

"Now think about the woman he loves—a beautiful, wealthy, smart young woman of twenty-eight. She has that extra spark that no one can quite explain. She's been through society's games and found them boring. Restless, she falls hard for him—and runs off to Europe to escape her feelings. But she's already back. It's only a matter of time before they end up together. Then they'll run away to Europe."

He walked even faster, thoughts racing.

"First, a massive scandal. After a year or two, she'll insist on coming back for the sake of his career. She won't be able to stand being an outsider. They'll go back and forth between countries, ruining their lives. His career will fall apart. Gossip and reporters will destroy them. It's the same old story."

He squeezed his fists tighter.

"And what about the children? Their mother locked up in an asylum. Their father living with another woman across the ocean. The whole world knowing the ugly truth. The kids will grow up bitter and broken. They'll never have a real chance at life."

He turned sharply and went back to the woman.

He pressed two fingers against her wrist, feeling her weak pulse.

"If she doesn't get morphine tonight, she'll die. One worthless life ends—and four others are saved."

His chest rose and fell heavily. His gray eyes seemed to smolder, like a silent, deadly weapon ready to strike. He said out loud:

"My God, what power! I hold five lives in my hands. I get to choose whether four people live good, full lives—or are destroyed forever. I could say like Nero once did, 'I am God.'"

He gave a cold, harsh laugh.

"I'm known for saving people when no one else could. They even joke that I've ruined the funeral business because I won't let people die. That's been my pride. Saving lives. But right now—right now—I've never felt prouder."

The woman on the bed suddenly twitched violently and opened her wild, desperate eyes.

"Give it to me—quick!" she gasped, her voice harsh and cracked.

"No," Blaine said calmly. "You're getting no more morphine. Not a single drop."

She stared at him, stunned. Then she let out a rough, ugly laugh.

"Stop joking," she growled. "Give it to me—quick—I'm so weak."

"No," he said again, his voice just as calm and firm.

He held her gaze, and slowly her eyes widened with fear. She pushed herself up on one arm.

"You really mean that?" she asked.

"Yes," he said.

He watched her closely, almost curious. She would be interesting to observe.

"You're going to cure me by force," she said, "since nothing else has worked?"

"Maybe," he answered.

Her face twisted with hatred. She had once been clever enough to realize he wasn't trying to help her—he was using her like an experiment. But she had also been strong-willed all her life, used to getting her way.

"Give me the morphine," she demanded sharply. "If you don't, I'll be dead by morning."

He stayed calm and unmoving.

She sprang off the bed and threw herself at him, filled with rage and fear.

"Give it to me!" she screamed. "Give it to me!" She tried to bite him.

He caught her by the shoulder and held her easily at arm's length. She twisted, kicked, and cursed, shrieking wild, filthy words like she had learned them in the streets. She clawed at the air, her nails slashing wildly. She looked like a crazed witch.

"What a beautiful bride she once was," the doctor thought. "And how many pages of useless praise have been written about her parties and charm."

The woman screamed louder.

"Give it to me, you monster! You devil! I always hated you! Give it to me! I'm dying! I'm dying! Help! Somebody help!" But the padded walls absorbed every sound. She knew no one would hear her.

He let her claw and strike at him, easily dodging her flailing arms and snapping teeth. He knew her pain was horrible. Her body was just a web of screaming nerves. Her sick mind could think of only one thing: getting the drug. She shook and twisted like a dying leaf about to fall from a tree. Her face, twisted and ugly, was full of tragedy.

The same desperate words kept coming from her dry throat: "Give me the morphine! Give me the morphine!"

Then, as she realized she couldn't break him, she tore away from him and ran wildly around the room, crying out in harsh, broken sounds. She yanked open the drawers of a dresser, throwing everything onto the floor, searching like a madwoman, her body jerking and trembling from the agony inside her.

The doctor watched, shivering at the sight, but he thought of the four innocent people whose lives were still trapped by her.

The woman finally collapsed onto the floor, biting the carpet, thrashing her arms uselessly, shredding her nightgown into pieces. She lay there shaking, looking like some awful, ruined thing that should have been sealed away next to ancient, broken statues.

Then she lifted herself on her hands and started crawling across the floor, slowly at first, like a man lost in the desert searching blindly for water.

The doctor, watching her closely, suddenly saw a flash of hope in her desperate eyes. She scrambled past him, heading straight for the washstand. Before he could guess what she was thinking, she grabbed a glass that had been left there and smashed it against the marble. He rushed forward just in time to stop her from cutting her own throat.

She looked up at him with a terrible, pleading expression.

"Please, give it to me!" she begged.

She clutched his knees, pressing her head against him. Her eyes were red and raw from the tears she couldn't shed. Her whole body stiffened and then collapsed.

"Poor creature," the doctor thought. "But what is one night of physical suffering compared to a lifetime of mental pain?"

"Just once!" she gasped. "Just once—or kill me!" Then, when he didn't move, she screamed again, "Kill me! Kill me!"

He picked her up, changed her into a clean nightgown, and laid her gently back on the bed. She stayed exactly where he placed her, too weak to move, her wide, blank eyes staring up at the ceiling above the large four-poster bed.

Blaine went back to his chair and checked his watch.

"She might live two more hours," he thought. "Maybe three. It's only midnight. There's plenty of time."

The room grew as silent as a mountain peak. He tried to read, but he couldn't focus. His mind was filled with the overwhelming sense of power. He was holding the future of four people in his hands.

Then fate, always unpredictable and cruel, played a dirty trick on him. His eyes wandered around the room and stopped on an old rocking chair. It looked familiar. After a moment, he realized why: it reminded him of the one his mother used to sit in.

She had been an invalid, and the purest, most selfless person he had ever known. He remembered, with a flicker of his old irritation, how her strict ideas of right and wrong had always frustrated him. Even as a good, honest boy, he had hated her endless moral lectures.

"Conscience," he had once snapped at her, "makes more women boring and more men failures than any ten crimes combined."

She had looked at him in horror and answered simply, "Conscience makes cowards of us all."

He lifted his head now with pride. The greatest achievement of modern civilization, he believed, was that smart men could overcome those old inherited feelings. Everyone had a conscience at first, but once the brain grew strong enough, it could strangle that little judge sitting in the back of the mind and throw it out.

Conscience? He hardly even remembered what that was anymore. He had never murdered anyone, never done anything truly dishonorable. If the urge had ever tempted him, his cold logic would have crushed it immediately. He had no problem pushing aside anyone who stood in his way. His work had required experiments that would have destroyed the nerves of a weaker man.

Conscience. What a nuisance, especially for someone planning a secret crime. How foolish it would be to be haunted by guilt afterward!

The woman groaned and twitched on the bed, pulling him back to the moment. He walked quickly over to her. Her face was dark with trapped blood, and her eyes were closed. He felt her pulse—it was weak.

"Not long now," he thought.

He moved back toward his chair, but suddenly felt a strong urge to keep walking. He began pacing the thick carpet more quickly than before.

"If I were an ordinary man," he told himself, "this would destroy me. But I'm not. If I let her live, she'll wreck four lives. If she dies, they'll be free."

The woman let out a horrible scream—like a soul being thrown into endless darkness. The silence before had been so total, the scream was shocking, horrible. Blaine jumped violently, and sweat broke out all over him.

"I'm a fool," he muttered, grateful to hear his own voice. "But I wish it were morning and the city noises had started."

He paced faster, stealing nervous glances at the bed. Even though the room was silent again, that awful scream echoed in his mind.

"Good God," he thought, "am I falling apart?"

He grabbed onto his thoughts like a drowning man.

"If I let her live," he reasoned, "a good man and a good woman will suffer. Two innocent children will be twisted forever. If I let her die, I save them all. Isn't that justice? Don't we sacrifice one criminal for the good of many? Isn't that exactly what the law does? It hangs a murderer to save society. I am simply carrying out that idea."

But a deep fear gnawed at him.

"Why am I hesitating? Is it—conscience? That useless feeling passed down by my ancestors? Something my mother fed and protected?"

He hated himself for feeling doubt. He fought it furiously.

"I will not hesitate," he told himself. "They must be saved, and I will do it. I must stay strong. I must prove my mind rules over all else."

Still, part of him quaked inside. He rushed over to the bed. Maybe she had already died? If so, he could just leave. He could run down the stairs, escape into the street. No one would ever know.

But when he bent over her, he saw she was still alive. She was breathing faintly, her mouth twisted in a cruel, mocking expression.

His hand went into his pocket. He pulled out a small case and opened it. Inside was a hypodermic syringe.

His fingers closed around it, and he started moving toward her. His muscles were so tight he thought he could hear them creak.

But at the last second, he stopped himself. He turned sharply away from the bed—and dropped the syringe onto the floor. Without thinking, he crushed it under his heel.

A Monarch of a Small Survey

I

The willows around the lake looked even sadder than they had forty years ago, when Dr. Hiram Webster had first bought the surrounding ranches from the old Moreño family. The Moreños were long gone, remembered only in the history books, but the willows and Dr. Webster were still standing, old and full of stories. The ranches had disappeared too, replaced by a sleepy city that only occasionally caught the energy of the busy metropolis across the bay.

Well-kept lawns stretched down to the lake. Big, fancy houses stood at the top of the lawns—homes of the city's wealthiest families. All the houses were owned by Dr. Webster, who rented them out for high prices to a lucky few. Living by Webster Lake meant you had social status, and it was worth dealing with whatever came along with it. Buying one of those pieces of land was about as likely as buying a house inside Yosemite National Park.

Webster Hall, the doctor's own home, was twenty years older than the surrounding mansions. Tall, thick trees crowded around it. When storms rolled in, the trees whipped the roof and howled with the wind. There was a strange, spooky feeling about the old, sprawling house. But no murders had happened there, no one had vanished into the trees without a trace, no ghost stories claimed it. Its mysterious air came simply from age—it was an ancient house in a young land. The lawns were overgrown, the windows stared blankly at the trees like empty eyes. Children ran past it quickly at night. People who didn't like the growing city said that if nothing creepy had happened there yet, it surely would someday—the house seemed destined for it.

One Sunday morning, rain poured down hard, pounding the patched-up tin roof and rushing loudly through the trees. Dr. Webster sat in a spinning chair at his desk, scowling. His wrinkled yellow face looked even more puckered than usual. He kept twisting around in his chair, glaring through the windows at the rain racing down the lawn into the lake. His mouth hung slightly open, and his clothes looked baggy on his thin frame. But his sharp black eyes still glittered with energy.

He grabbed a large bell from the desk and rang it loudly. A maid quickly appeared.

"Go check the barometer," he shouted. "See if this damned rain plans on stopping."

The maid disappeared and came back a minute later to say the barometer didn't show any sign of change.

"Fine," he barked. "Set the table for twenty anyway! If they don't show up, I'll raise their rent. Send Miss Webster to me."

A few minutes later, his sister walked in. She was almost as old as he was, but her faded face only showed wrinkles on her forehead and around her eyes. There was still something young and hopeful about her, like a woman who had aged against her will and hadn't quite accepted it yet. Her hair was neatly styled, but she wore a worn black silk dress, with just a small hair brooch for decoration. Her hands were small and carefully kept, although the skin was loose and spotted with age. She stood straight, but she was thick around the waist.

"What is it, brother?" she asked softly, speaking to the back of his chair.

He spun around sharply.

"Why do you always sneak in like a cat? Do you think those people will come today? It's raining cats and dogs."

"Of course they'll come," she said. "They always do, and they all have carriages."

"That's the problem," he grumbled. "They're getting too fancy. Soon they'll think they don't need me anymore. But if they do, I'll throw them all out."

"They treat you the same way they always have, Hiram," she said patiently.

"You think so? You really think they'll come today?"

"I'm sure they will, Hiram."

He looked her up and down for a moment, then surprised her by softening his voice with a rare touch of kindness.

"You need a new dress, Marian," he said. "That one's getting old."

If Dr. Webster had any sense of humor, he might have laughed at the shocked look on his sister's face. She hurried over and placed her hand on his shoulder.

"Hiram," she said, worried, "are you... you don't look well today."

"I'm fine," he said, shaking her hand off. "But I've noticed you and Abigail are starting to look shabby, and I don't want those fancy folks criticizing you."

He opened his desk, pulled out four twenty-dollar gold coins, and placed them in her hand.

"Will this be enough? I don't know anything about women's clothes."

Miss Webster, grateful to get any money without a long argument, quickly assured him it was enough. She left the room right away to find her companion, Miss Williams.

Miss Williams was sitting on the edge of her bed in her small, plain room, staring out through the rain and trees, just like Dr. Webster was doing downstairs. She had sat like this on the night she first arrived at Webster Hall, an eighteen-year-old girl full of dreams. She had sat like this many times since, feeling her youth slip away, silently protesting the dull, empty life she lived, yet too timid and unsure to leave and chase something better.

Today was her birthday. She had just turned forty-two. She kept asking herself the same question she had asked before: why had she stayed? Deep down, had she hoped that the old Websters would die and leave her enough money to finally live freely, to travel and enjoy life?

She loved Miss Webster and had been happy to leave the small New England town where she had been a charity case among relatives. Miss Webster needed a companion and housekeeper—there was no salary, but she had been promised a safe home and nice clothes, and the satisfaction of earning them herself. She had come full of youth, spirit, and hope. Now, all of that was gone.

Today, she wished she had married any ordinary man back in her hometown—anyone who had been kind enough to offer. She had never known real freedom, or love, or the feeling of living her own life.

Miss Webster suddenly entered the room.

"Abby," she said, a little breathless, "Hiram is sick." She quickly explained how her brother had shown rare kindness earlier.

Miss Williams barely reacted. She was so tired of hearing about Hiram. She thanked Miss Webster without much feeling when she was handed a gold coin. In her mind, a bitter phrase repeated over and over: You're forty-two. You're old. You're nobody.

"What's wrong?" Miss Webster asked kindly. "Have you been crying? Are you feeling sick? You'd better get dressed, dear. The guests will be arriving soon."

She suddenly sat down next to Abby and hugged her tightly, tears springing to her eyes.

"We're old women," she said sadly. "Life hasn't given us much, has it? You're younger, but you've given all your best years to this gloomy old house. You have no more youth left than we do. Poor girl!"

The two women held each other close for a moment. Abby realized that, even if Miss Webster wasn't a very deep person, she still had regrets—still longed for the life she had missed.

"It's strange," Miss Webster went on, "how we only get one chance to be young. And it often comes when we're too poor or too busy to enjoy it. I spent my youth working, working, working. Now that I have time to meet people, it's too late. But you—you're still young compared to me. You still have time. You could live another thirty years."

She paused, her voice full of longing. "Oh, if only I had those thirty years!"

"I would give them to you gladly," Abby said, "if I could have just one year of happiness and youth."

Miss Webster stood up and wiped her eyes.

"Well," she said, trying to sound cheerful, "crying won't change anything. We have guests to entertain today. Put on your best dress, dear, and come down."

She left the room.

Abby quickly took a brown silk dress from her closet and slipped it on. Her hair was always neat, parted with a sharp white line that curved down to the braids pinned at the back of her neck.

As she looked in the mirror today, she had a sudden, reckless thought: she wanted to cut a fringe into her hair, maybe even put some color on her cheeks—anything to bring back a trace of the pretty young girl she used to be. She picked up a pair of scissors but dropped them just as fast. She didn't have the courage. She could already imagine the mocking stares, the whispered comments, the harsh judgment from old Dr. Webster.

She stared hard at her reflection, trying to picture herself with a softer hairstyle. It wouldn't erase the lines around her eyes and mouth, but at least it could hide her aging forehead. Her cheeks were thin and pale, but her skin was still smooth. Her once-dark blue eyes had faded, but they hadn't lost their spirit yet. Her lips had lost their fullness, but her teeth were still good. Her head was well-shaped and sat proudly on her shoulders, even if her figure had thickened and lost its curves under the stiff brown dress.

If she had been rich, she might have looked youthful and lovely at forty-two. But instead, she was just another old maid, her fine features wasted.

Abby went downstairs to take her usual place in the parlor and later at the dinner table—always invisible to the fancy guests who never cared to notice the Websters' companion. She hated them all. She took a mean kind of pleasure in seeing them age, too, even though she knew it was wrong. Even with all their money, they hadn't kept what she believed she could have kept, if only she'd had the chance.

The first carriage pulled up just as she reached the bottom of the stairs. The maid had opened the door wide, and rain splashed in. There was no covered entryway, so the guests had to run up the steps to keep from getting soaked. Mrs. Holt, one of the most fashionable women in town, dragged her skirts through the puddles and cursed Dr. Webster under her breath.

"I'll be the happiest woman alive when these dinners are finally over," Mrs. Holt muttered under her breath. "Thank goodness, he can't live much longer!"

"Hush!" her cautious husband whispered as Miss Webster appeared.

Miss Webster and Mrs. Holt greeted each other warmly, kissing each other's cheeks. Everyone liked Miss Webster. Mrs. Holt, who carried herself stiffly with the pride of new money, held Miss Webster's hand in both of hers and assured her that no storm could keep her from attending one of dear Dr. Webster's famous Sunday dinners. But as she went upstairs to take off her wet coat, she couldn't help but frown at a strange painting of the doctor dressed in Japanese robes that hung on the wall.

Other guests arrived, and after making their way upstairs to leave their coats, they gathered in the parlor to wait for the doctor. The room was dark and gloomy. Outside, the trees thrashed against the rain-soaked windows. The carpet inside was worn thin. The heavy black furniture was covered with neat white crocheted covers, but that just made everything look even more grim. A table with a marble top stood in the middle like a tombstone, topped by a glass case containing wax flowers. On the walls were faded family photos in narrow gold frames. In a place of honor hung the doctor's diploma; nearby was Miss Webster's first stitched sampler. In the corner stood "the first piano ever brought to California," which looked more like the ghost of a piano than an actual instrument. Miss Williams half expected one of its legs to fall off one day.

Miss Webster sat stiffly in a tall-backed chair by the table, doing her best to chat with her guests. The women huddled together for warmth, not caring if they wrinkled their expensive dresses. The men stood off to one side, grumbling about the old-fashioned midday dinner they were about to endure.

Miss Williams sank into a chair and stared blankly around the room. She had sat through this same scene nearly every week for twenty-five years. Today, a sharp pang of relief hit her when she noticed something different—there was a young person among them. Usually, no amount of threats or begging could bring young people to Webster Hall. And to her surprise, it was a young man, not a girl. She wasn't in the mood to see a fresh, hopeful girl today.

The young man was tall and lean, with the easy strength of a college athlete and an open, friendly face. He stood awkwardly, his hands stuffed in his pockets, looking around the gloomy room in obvious shock. After a moment, he caught Miss Williams's eye. She smiled without meaning to, feeling something warm and alive stir inside her. He immediately walked over to her.

"I say," he said, a little sheepishly, "I haven't been introduced yet, but do you mind if we skip that and just talk? I've never seen so many old fogies in one room, and this place feels like a funeral parlor. I keep thinking someone's going to sneak up behind me!"

Miss Williams felt a sudden, grateful flutter in her chest.

"Sit down," she said with a spark of energy she didn't know she still had. "How did you end up here?"

"Well, you see, I'm staying with the Holts. Jack Holt and I were college roommates. They told me I should visit the oldest house in the city and meet the most famous man on this side of the bay, so I said sure. But good grief, I didn't expect this. Jack said nothing on earth could get him through the door here. Since it's my first trip to California, I figured I ought to see all the sights. What about you?"

"I live here," she said. "I've lived here for twenty-four years."

"Good Lord!" he burst out, his eyes wide. "You've lived in this house for twenty-four years?"

"Twenty-four years."

"And you're still alive? Sorry—" he quickly added, realizing how rude he sounded.

She gave a small, genuine laugh. "No offense taken. I'm glad you understand just how dreadful it is. Most people don't. They've known me for years, but they never seem to wonder how I survive it. You know, you're the first young person I've spoken to in years—years."

"You're joking," he said, shocked and full of pity. "I'd have run away long ago."

"What would be the point?" she said quietly. "I stayed too long. I'm an old woman now. Might as well stay until the end."

The young man looked uncomfortable, but before he could reply, Dr. Webster entered the room.

The old man wore shiny, old-fashioned black clothes, likely made by a tailor long dead. He leaned heavily on a gold-topped cane.

"Howdy, howdy, howdy!" he shouted, his voice rough but friendly. "Glad to see you. Thought you wouldn't come—but I knew you would!" He chuckled. "Come on, let's eat. I'm starving."

Without greeting anyone individually, he turned and led them through the hall and down a narrow, creaky staircase into the basement dining room. It was just as gloomy as the parlor, though the silver on the table was heavy and the linen was some of the finest you could find anywhere.

The guests sat wherever they wanted, with the young man sticking close to Miss Williams. Dr. Webster quickly started serving the soup, grumbling that he felt like letting everyone serve themselves because he was so hungry. After quickly handing out a few bowls, he helped himself straight from the big tureen.

"Old brute," muttered Mrs. Holt under her breath. "It's disgusting that he's so rich he can do whatever he wants."

Aside from her comment, the first course passed in heavy silence. No one dared say much unless Dr. Webster started the conversation— and he was too busy eating.

When the soup was cleared, a huge dinner was laid out. Dr. Webster, who was normally stingy, spared no expense in the kitchen. But the guests didn't feel like celebrating. They sighed to themselves, knowing they would be expected to eat a mountain of food in the middle of the day.

The doctor carved the turkeys, serving everyone generous slices. After finishing his own plate, he finally began to talk.

"Cleveland's going to win the election," he said loudly. "You hear me? Harrison doesn't stand a chance. What was that?" His thick eyebrows pulled together sharply. He had caught a whisper of disagreement. "Did you say he wouldn't win, John Holt?"

"No, no," Mr. Holt said quickly—he was a strong Republican but didn't dare argue. "Cleveland will definitely be re-elected."

"Well, you better remember it!" the doctor barked. "I'll find out how you vote, don't think I won't! If you dare vote Republican—" He snapped his teeth together in a sharp, threatening click. Holt nervously raised his wine glass. Dr. Webster still held a large debt over him.

"The Republican party is dead—dead as a doornail," added a heavyset man with a sly, agreeable smile, trying to please the doctor. "Don't worry about it, doctor. By the way, what do you think about the wheat crops?"

"Never better, never better," Dr. Webster said. "They're saying the Northern crops will fail, but that's a lie. They'll be just fine. Don't worry, Meeker. And wipe that long face off—I don't like it."

"The reports haven't been great," began a gloomy-looking man.

"Don't argue with me!" the doctor shouted. "I said the crops won't fail. They haven't for eight years—why would they now?"

"No reason at all, sir," the man said quickly, eager to calm him down. "It's good to hear your predictions."

"I hear Consolidated Virginia is going up," Mrs. Holt said, trying to change the subject politely.

"Nonsense!" Dr. Webster shouted, slamming his heavy silver fork onto his plate. "That mine's worthless! Nothing but dirt left. No more fools are going to get rich off it. You haven't put money in it, have you? If you have, don't ever come back here!"

Everyone quickly assured him that none of their money had gone into the stock market.

"Wow," the young man whispered to Miss Williams, "does he always act like this? And do these people just sit there and take it?"

"They're used to it," she whispered back. "He's made this area so exclusive that living here gives them social status. Since he refuses to sell the houses, they have no choice but to put up with him. Plus, they all hope he'll leave the houses to them when he dies. They've been putting up with this for years—dragging themselves here through rain or shine, eating this awful midday dinner, listening to his endless old stories about early California. They never argue with him. Not once. They thought he'd die long ago, but now they're trapped—and even if they wanted to stand up to him, they wouldn't know how anymore."

"That's disgusting," the young man muttered.

His independent spirit made Miss Williams admire him even more.

"I'd love to stand up to him," he said.

"Oh, please don't!" she whispered, scared.

She was dreading the moment Dr. Webster would notice the newcomer.

The young man laughed softly. "Why are you so scared of him? He doesn't beat you, does he?"

"It's not that," she said. "It's just who he is. And we're all so used to it."

Suddenly, Dr. Webster turned and barked, "Well, Mr. Strowbridge, what are you doing with your life? I hear you just got out of Harvard. University men never amount to anything."

Strowbridge's face turned red, but he kept calm.

"University men," the doctor went on, "don't even learn anything now. Just football and rowing. Think that'll earn you a living out here? Got any money of your own?"

"My father, since you ask, is a wealthy man—and a gentleman," Strowbridge said, struggling to keep his voice steady. "He inherited his money. He didn't have to come to a new country and turn into a savage."

Mr. Holt, panicking, kicked Strowbridge under the table, but it was too late. Miss Williams sat frozen, both terrified and thrilled. The other guests stared in horror. For the first time ever, someone had dared to talk back to the master of Webster Hall.

"Sir! Sir!" Webster sputtered, then roared, "Who invited this cub here? Who gave you permission to bring friends into my house? How dare you speak to me like that? Do you know who I am—?"

"Oh, I know," Strowbridge interrupted, his young temper fully unleashed. "You're a rude, arrogant old man who wouldn't be accepted anywhere if it weren't for your money." He pushed his chair back and stood up. "Good day to you, sir. I pity you. You have no real friends. I'm sorry for being rude—but honestly, I couldn't help it."

And with that, he marched out of the room.

For Miss Williams, it felt like all the light left the room when the young man walked out. The shocked guests immediately threw themselves into eating, almost desperately. Dr. Webster just sat there, staring blankly at the door. His food made a grinding noise in his mouth, like stones in a machine. He didn't speak for a long time. When he finally did, he acted like nothing had happened with young Strowbridge. His tone was noticeably calmer—almost dazed—but he didn't seem completely defeated.

The long, heavy dinner dragged on until it finally ended. The women went back upstairs to the front parlor to sip tea with Miss Webster and awkwardly shift around on the stiff old furniture. The men followed Dr. Webster into the billiard room. Even though they were tired and sluggish, they spent three hours taking turns playing and listening to the old man's endless stories about his younger days fighting grizzly bears. It was clear he was trying hard to remind everyone of how tough he had once been.

That night, lying in the big old four-poster bed where he had been born, surrounded by the heavy, ugly furniture brought from his New England home, Dr. Webster quietly died.

II

Everyone with any social standing in the city came to Dr. Webster's funeral. There had never been so many serious faces and people dressed in black. Since Miss Webster was too overwhelmed with grief to attend, Miss Williams handled everything. The families who lived by the lake were given special seats at the front, just beyond the expensive casket. Their faces were hard to read. After Miss Williams spoke quietly with each of them, Strowbridge stepped forward and whispered in her ear.

"I just have to tell someone in the family how sorry I am for losing my temper the other day. It was really rude of me. Poor old man! Please forgive me."

A small smile crossed Miss Williams' tired face.

"He had a good heart," she said. "He would have forgiven you."

Then the long, solemn ceremony began.

Everyone followed the hearse to the cemetery, even though it was pouring rain. Miss Williams, as the main mourner, rode alone in a carriage right behind the hearse. During the long, dreary ride, she fought hard to push down an inappropriate feeling of hope. In the other carriages, the talk was less restrained. People were already whispering about their expectations.

Two days later, the crowd of tired businesspeople boarded the usual evening train. The newsboys were shouting excitedly, waving papers in the air.

"Will of Dr. Hiram Webster! Full account of Dr. Webster's last will and testament!"

Within moments, newspapers were opened everywhere. After five minutes, they were scattered all over the floor, along with peanut shells and orange peels. A heavy silence hung over the train—then bursts of angry conversation. Only a handful of people sat frozen with pale faces—the residents of Webster Lake.

Dr. Webster had left every penny to his sister.

For two weeks, no one from the lake went to visit Miss Webster. They were too upset. But after a while, common sense—and ambition—pushed them to return. After all, Miss Webster now had millions, and she would have to make her own will one day.

When they finally called on her, she welcomed them kindly. Her eyes were red from crying, but they couldn't help noticing how rich her black mourning clothes looked—nicer than anything they had ever seen her wear before. They also noticed how proudly she held her head now, something new in her manner. She didn't exactly look down on them, but it was clear she understood the power her fortune gave her.

Meanwhile, Strowbridge looked around for Miss Williams. Not seeing her in the parlor, he wandered outside and spotted her coming from the dairy. She wore a plain black dress and a dark apron, and her face looked tired and sad.

"She looks so hopeless," he thought angrily. "That selfish old man could have left her something so she could finally live her life."

When she saw him, she brightened and hurried down the path. They sat on the steps and talked quietly. She admitted she had been deeply disappointed to find herself still tied to the old house, still a servant, still stuck. She confessed she dreamed of traveling, seeing all the places she had only read about. Later, she would blush with shame at how openly she had spoken. She, who was always so guarded, had opened up to a stranger—but he had been so kind.

As the visitors left that day, their comments were sharp.

"I do believe Marian Webster is going to get stuck-up now," said Mrs. Holt.

"Well, four million dollars is a pretty good excuse," sighed Mrs. Meeker.

"That dress must have cost at least three hundred dollars!" said another. "She's clearly open to new ideas now."

But Miss Webster wasn't done surprising them. A month later, Mrs. Meeker burst into Mrs. Holt's house, breathless.

"You won't believe it!" she cried. "Miss Webster is redecorating the whole house—everything!"

She explained how the workers were everywhere, painting, pulling up old carpets, and installing new ones. Miss Webster had even asked everyone to stay away until it was finished.

"Can you imagine that old tomb being turned into something modern?" Mrs. Holt gasped. "Hiram Webster will haunt the place!"

But Miss Webster had waited a long time for this moment. The shock of her new wealth had pushed grief aside and filled her head with endless possibilities. She had no desire to travel anymore, but she had always longed for luxury—and now, at last, she could have it. She told Miss Williams that she might not have many years left, but she intended to enjoy every one of them.

Before long, all the important families of the city received fancy invitations bordered in black, announcing that Miss Webster would be receiving guests at four o'clock every Thursday.

On the first Thursday, the parlor of Webster Hall was crowded, just like it had been at the funeral. But now, no one could recognize the place.

"Who would have thought it?" they whispered.

Elegant lace covered the windows, heavy blue satin framed them. The walls were painted with pink angels floating on soft clouds. The floor was covered in thick blue velvet carpet. The chairs and couches were deep and soft, and even the doorways were draped in blue satin. The woodwork gleamed silver. In the hall, Persian rugs lay across the polished floors, and rich tapestries lined the walls. Carved furniture filled the corners. Through the open doors of the library, guests could see leather-covered walls, marble busts, and low bookcases. Even an old laboratory had been turned into a luxurious dining room where a fancy lunch was served.

Miss Webster proudly led the lakeside guests upstairs. Every spare bedroom had been decorated in a fancy, colorful style. When they were finally allowed to step into Miss Webster's own bedroom, their mouths dropped open in shock. The surprise alone kept them from laughing out loud.

The room looked like it belonged to a young, spoiled princess. The walls were covered in shimmering pink silk under delicate lace. The white enamel bed and dressing table were wrapped with the same pink and white materials. Pink light poured through silky curtains. The white carpet was scattered with pink roses. On the dressing table, everything was crystal and gold. A tall Psyche mirror stood in one corner. Two lamps, both shaded in pink, glowed softly.

Everyone saw how over-the-top it was, but no one noticed how sad it really was underneath.

The doctor's old room had been left exactly the same. Sentimental value—and the worth of the old mahogany furniture—had saved it. Miss Williams's room was still the same tiny cell it had always been. She helped greet the guests, wearing a new black silk dress. Miss Webster herself wore a full English crêpe outfit with a wide collar and a jet-black belt.

That day became one of the most talked-about events in the city's history.

From then on, Miss Webster hosted a fancy dinner party every Sunday evening at seven. This time, no one dared to grumble about the invitations. No single woman had ever gotten so much attention before.

At each dinner, Miss Webster wore a new outfit. By the third dinner, she stunned everyone by showing up with enormous diamond earrings. By the fourth, people whispered that she had been getting her nails professionally manicured. By the fifth, it was obvious she had started wearing a corset. At the sixth dinner, they stared in shock—Miss

Webster was wearing makeup. But by the tenth dinner, they were completely speechless: Miss Webster had a blond wig.

"They can talk all they want," Miss Webster said to her companion that night, sitting before her mirror and inspecting her heavily made-up face. "I have four million dollars, and I'll do whatever I please. It's the first time in my life I can, and I intend to enjoy every single moment. Whose business is it, anyway?"

"No one's," said Miss Williams carefully. "But you have to expect people to talk. It does seem a little... ridiculous."

"They'd better talk!" snapped Miss Webster, showing a flash of the tough personality once only seen in her brother. "And why is it ridiculous? Doesn't a woman have the right to be young if she can? I was a faithful sister to Hiram, but he took away my youth. Now that he's given me the means to get it back, I'm going to make the most of it."

"You can't really be young again," Miss Williams said quietly.

"Maybe not by years," said Miss Webster, "but I can still have everything youth brings."

"Not everything," her companion replied. "No man will fall in love with you."

Miss Webster snapped her false teeth together sharply. "And why not? What difference do a few years make? Seventy isn't much when you think about it! Think about people starving with just seventy dollars. Or how many thousands of years old the earth is! I have everything now that makes a woman desirable—money, beauty, perfect care. Even the steam treatments are smoothing out my wrinkles! I can see it."

She turned from the mirror and gave Miss Williams a resentful look.

"But I wish I had your extra thirty years. I do! I do! Then everyone would see."

For a long moment, the two women stared at each other in silence. Whatever love or friendship they once had was gone. In its place, hidden but growing, was resentment and bitterness. Miss Webster deeply envied Miss Williams's youth, even if it was fading. Miss Williams, in turn, deeply envied the older woman's new power—her money, her freedom to chase after what she wanted.

That night, Miss Williams cried hard into her pillow.

"I'm leaving," she whispered to herself. "I'll work as a servant somewhere else if I have to. But I can't stay here any longer."

The next morning, she stood on the front porch and watched Miss Webster leave for the market. The carriage and horses were the best in California. The coachman and footman wore full uniforms. Miss Webster sat proudly inside, dressed in a black silk gown covered in shiny black beads. A huge hat covered with feathers sat firmly on top of her red wig, held in place by a thick, dotted veil. She carried a black lace parasol and wore polished patent leather shoes, her small foot peeking out as she stepped up.

"The old fool," muttered Abby. "Why couldn't it have been me? I could've made myself look young without being ridiculous."

She let her chores slide and wandered down to the lake. Brightly painted boats were tied up near fancy boat houses. They looked strange under the drooping old willows. The lawns were bright green, fresh with spring. Roses grew wildly everywhere. The windows of the big, old-fashioned houses were open. Abby caught glimpses of girls in white dresses, heard the plinking of a mandolin, the sharp, careful notes of a piano, and the sudden rise of a clear young voice singing.

"After all," she thought with a sigh, "it doesn't seem to matter much to them that they didn't inherit anything."

A young man stepped out of one of the big windows of the Holt mansion and walked across the lawn. Abby recognized him—Strowbridge. She hadn't seen him in weeks, but she had thought about him during her darker days. Her heart jumped when she saw him now.

"I'm such a fool," she thought. "Even if I had her money, it wouldn't matter. I'm nearly twice his age."

He hopped into a boat and started rowing across the lake. When he passed the Webster property, he spotted her.

"Hey there!" he called out like she was a teenager. "How've you been? Come take a ride with me!"

He quickly brought the boat to shore and offered his hand like he expected her to say yes. Abby didn't resist. She stepped lightly into the boat, and soon they were gliding across the water. She admired his strong young figure, dressed casually in a sweater and white pants. His blue eyes peeked out under a yachting cap, and his face was tanned from the sun. Abby wondered if many young men were as handsome as he was. In truth, he was just a typical, healthy young American whose charm came from his kindness and openness.

"Nice, isn't it?" he asked, smiling into her eyes.

"Very much," she said. "Hiram used to row us sometimes, but he'd get so mad that the boat rocked, and I was always scared we'd tip over."

"Hiram must've been a real terror," he laughed.

"A what?"

"Sorry! I guess you don't know much slang. Bad habit of mine."

He rowed back and forth across the lake, sometimes letting the boat drift where the willow branches met overhead. He talked the whole time—telling her about his college days, boat races, and football games he played in. At first, he just wanted to cheer up the lonely woman. But she was such a good listener, so eager and warm, that he forgot he was supposed to pity her.

An hour passed, and with it, her bitterness. She no longer felt trapped at Webster Hall. But remembering her duties, she reluctantly asked him to take her back.

"If you must," he said. "But I'm sorry. We'll have to do this again sometime. Thanks so much for coming."

"Thank me?" she said, laughing lightly as she stepped onto the shore. "Oh, you have no idea—"

She hurried up the path, smiling.

Miss Webster was standing on the porch, her face twisted in an angry frown.

"Well!" she snapped. "Off flirting with boys at your age! Aren't you ashamed of yourself?"

It felt like Abby had been slapped. But a new spirit—one touched by the kindness she'd just been shown—rose inside her.

"Wouldn't you have gone if he'd asked you?" Abby shot back.

Miss Webster turned her back and stormed inside to her room. She locked the door and broke down in tears.

"I can't help it," she sobbed. "It's terrible to hate Abby after all these years, but those awful thirty years between us! I'd give three million dollars to be where she is. I used to think she was old too—but she isn't. She's young! A baby compared to me! I could be her mother! Oh, I must pray and try to get rid of these feelings."

She wrote a check to her pastor and called for the trained nurse from New York. She demanded to be steamed, massaged, and rubbed with lotions and wine to restore her aging body.

Meanwhile, Strowbridge made it a habit to drop by and visit Miss Williams whenever he could. Sometimes he found her at the dairy, sitting on a table corner while she worked on the butter. He liked her old-fashioned music and often got her to play the grand piano in the fancy blue parlor. He brought her new books too, mostly stories about men by male writers. He had no patience for books full of romance or drama.

Even Miss Webster grew to like him, partly because he didn't give her the chance not to, and partly because his lively personality was impossible to resist. She even invited him to dinner once in a while. Eventually, he joked with her like she was a schoolgirl, which made her feel young again.

As for Abby, he was truly fond of her.

"You're such good company, you know," he told her. "Most girls are boring. They don't know anything and just want to be flirted with. But you—you're like another fellow, you know."

"I'm used to being a companion," she said with a small smile.

When June came, Strowbridge went back to Boston—and for one woman, the world seemed a lot dimmer.

Life at Webster Hall continued. People got used to seeing Miss Webster acting younger and younger. They even stopped pretending to flatter her. No men proposed, even with her fortune. The gap between the two women grew wider. Every week, Abby promised herself she would leave. Every week, Miss Webster vowed to kick her out. But neither could actually do it. Habit and dependence tied them together.

The next summer, Strowbridge returned. Almost right away, he went to see Miss Williams.

"I feel like you're one of the best friends I've got," he said warmly, sitting beside her on the porch. "And—I brought you a little gift, if you don't mind."

He pulled a small case from his pocket and opened it to reveal a tiny gold watch with a fob.

"You know," he'd told himself while buying it, "she's so much older, it's not improper. It's just a gift for a good friend. Poor old thing!"

Still, he looked at her a little nervously, worried about how she might react.

His worries turned out to be nothing. Abby looked at the small, beautiful gift with a bright, shining face.

"For me?" she cried. "That lovely thing is really for me?"

"Of course it is," he said, feeling relieved and not noticing how much her happiness meant. "You'll accept it, right?"

"I certainly will," she said, placing it gently on her palm and admiring it. She pinned the fob to her blouse for a moment, but then shook her head and took it off. "I'll just keep it to admire and only wear it with my black silk dress. It's too nice for this old worn-out alpaca."

"What a stingy old woman the Circus must—"

"Shhh! Don't say that. She might hear you," Abby said quickly. "Let's go walk in the garden."

They wandered through the neatly kept lawns and colorful flower beds until they reached a long path lined with fig trees. The branches were full of big green leaves and heavy purple fruit. Abby opened one of the figs and showed him the juicy red center.

"You don't have these back East," she said.

"We don't. Can you eat them just like that?"

She smiled and held a fig half up to his mouth.

"Eat!" she said.

And he did. Then he ate a dozen more as she opened them for him.

"I feel like a greedy schoolboy," he laughed. "But they're amazing. You've introduced me to a new favorite."

"Now let's go take a row on the lake," he suggested.

All that afternoon, Abby forgot the years that had passed. In her mind, she felt as young as she had been when she first arrived at Webster Hall. That night, she knelt by her bed, pressing her hands against her face.

"I know I'm being foolish," she thought. "But things like this have happened before. If only I had a little of her money."

The next day she wandered down to the lake, telling herself she wasn't expecting him to invite her out again—she just wanted to see him. She spotted him quickly. He was rowing with Elinor Holt, the prettiest girl on the lakeside. His eyes were locked on Elinor's smiling face. He didn't even glance at Abby.

She turned and walked back to the house, feeling like her body was frozen and only an invisible force was pushing her forward. But as soon as she got inside, she threw herself into her busy household duties. When she finally had time to think, the sadness returned.

"I'm a fool," she thought. "Of course he would pay attention to Elinor Holt. She's his host's daughter. But still—he could have looked up."

That night she couldn't sleep. As she lay awake, strange noises drifted into her room from the hallway. She got up quietly and opened her door a crack.

Out in the dim hall, she saw a white figure moving back and forth, wringing its hands. Gray hair shook wildly around a trembling head.

"No use!" the figure moaned. "No use, no use! I'm old, old, old! Seventy-four, seventy-four, seventy-four! Oh Lord, oh Lord, oh Lord! Your ways are too mysterious for us to understand. Amen!"

Abby quickly shut her door. She knew whatever was happening out there was too sad and private to witness. She listened as the figure moved closer and lightly tapped on her door.

"Give me back those thirty years!" the old voice whimpered. "They're mine! You stole them!"

Abby felt her hair stand on end.

"Is Marian losing her mind?" she wondered in fear.

But the next morning, Miss Webster looked the same as always when she finally came down after her late breakfast. She was all dressed up for her trip to the market. She had given up full mourning clothes and now wore a lavender dress, with a matching hat and parasol—everything matching, that is, except herself.

"Poor old parody," Abby thought sadly. "She makes me feel young."

A week later, when the maid went into Miss Webster's room at the usual time, she found the bed empty. Miss Webster was nowhere to be seen. Alarmed, she ran to tell Abby, and together they searched the house.

They finally found her—in her brother's old bedroom, lying peacefully in the same big mahogany bed where she had been born. She was dead. Her gray hair was smoothed neatly under a lace nightcap, and her hands were folded neatly over her chest, the nails still shining in the dim light.

Death had come quietly to her, just as it had to her brother. Why she had chosen to return to that room at the end was the last mystery her strange old heart left behind.

III

There was another funeral at the old house, and again a crowd of mourners gathered. This time, though, there was less showy sadness— there wasn't anyone left they needed to impress. The lakeside neighbors grouped together at the far end of the parlor and talked openly.

"Miss Williams should have put the blond wig on her," Mrs. Holt whispered. "I'm sure Marian would have done that for herself. Poor Marian! She really was a good soul, and she gave a lot to charity. I wonder if she left anything to Miss Williams?"

"Of course she did. Miss Williams deserves a good share," someone replied.

It was an obvious point. The women exchanged knowing looks. No more words were needed, but Mrs. Holt added anyway:

"I think we can count on getting our houses now. Marian really did like us, and she didn't have any family. But just to be safe, I'm going to make sure I get a keepsake from the famous Webster place."

She opened a cabinet, pulled out a small antique teapot, and casually slipped it into her bag.

The others laughed silently.

"That's just like you," said Mrs. Meeker, smiling.

Then all conversation stopped as the ceremony began and they bowed their heads respectfully.

Two days later, Miss Williams wandered up and down the hall, waiting anxiously for the evening paper. This time, she didn't pretend to herself—she admitted she was eager to know what Marian had left her. She still felt fondness for the woman who had been a part of her life for so long, but she was honest about her excitement for what the future might bring.

Several times she had thought about leaving and finding a hotel, but even though she hated the old house, the years she had spent there held her back. She felt like she couldn't leave until the law officially told her she had to.

"I won't get the full inheritance for about ten months," she thought. "But I'll have the income. I can even borrow if I need to. Maybe I'll live in the city... or maybe—no, I shouldn't think about that yet."

At that moment, a newsboy appeared at the end of the walkway. His arms were full of newspapers. He quickly rolled one up and tossed it expertly toward her. Miss Williams couldn't wait any longer. She ran down the path, caught the paper, and rushed back upstairs to her room, locking the door behind her.

For a moment, she felt dizzy. Then she shook the newspaper open with trembling hands. She didn't have to search far. The will of such an important figure as Miss Webster was printed right on the front page. A whole column was devoted to it, and the details were spelled out clearly in bold headlines.

MISS MARIAN WEBSTER'S WILL

———

SHE GIVES HER ENTIRE FORTUNE TO CHARITY

———

FOUR MILLION DOLLARS EXCHANGED FOR EVERLASTING FAME

———

NO INHERITANCES LEFT BEHIND

The room spun around the forgotten woman. She felt sick, then cold all the way to her bones. She collapsed to the floor, clutching the newspaper. After a while, she spread it out and forced herself to read through the blurred words. Her name wasn't mentioned anywhere. All those years of loyalty had meant nothing. Thirty years of silent resentment had won in the end. It was Miss Webster's final act of revenge.

No tears came to Abby's eyes. She just gasped now and then. "How could she? How could she? How could she?" her mind kept repeating. "What difference would it have made to her after she was dead? And me—oh God—what will happen to me?"

For a while she didn't even think about Strowbridge. When she finally did, she pictured him smiling at Elinor Holt. The fantasy she had built around him crumbled in that moment of cruel reality. Even if she had seen an announcement of his engagement in the paper, it would not have surprised her now. Everything made sense—how he had acted, how everything had lined up—and it was all clear he belonged to Elinor.

"Fool! Fool!" she cried silently. "But no—thank God, at least I had that one sweet dream, the only one in forty-three years!"

A maid knocked on her door to call her to dinner. Abby told her to go away. She stayed curled up on the floor for hours, locked in darkness. The stars shone outside, but the wind whipped the lake and slammed the tree branches against the roof.

When half the night had passed, Abby finally struggled to her feet. Her body was stiff and aching. She opened the door and listened. The house was dark and silent. She shuffled over to Miss Webster's room. It was just as empty.

She lit the lamps and filled the room with soft pink light. She let down her hair and, using Miss Webster's old scissors, cut herself a thick fringe of bangs. Her hair fell softly, but the part down the middle was obvious and awkward.

On the dressing table was a bottle of gum tragacanth. She used it to glue the stray hair into place, making the bangs look even. It hid her tired forehead, but her face was still pale and worn out.

She knew where Miss Webster kept her cosmetics. A few minutes later, jars and bottles covered the table.

She painted her face white, added some red to her cheeks, darkened her eyelashes, and brightened her lips with rouge. She twisted her hair into a loose bun. Then she slipped off her black dress and pulled on a stunning white satin evening gown from the closet.

The square neckline was filled with lace, hiding her thin neck. She squeezed into French slippers and tugged long gloves over her arms. Then she stared at herself in the tall Psyche mirror.

Her eyes lit up. Under the soft light and makeup, she almost looked young again. She was almost beautiful.

"This is what I could have looked like if I had money when I was young," she said to the reflection. "I wouldn't have needed all this paint for years yet if I'd had the chance to take care of myself. Even now—even now—if I had money and happiness!"

She leaned closer to the mirror, pressing her finger against the glass. Her voice was steady, without anger:

"When that letter came twenty-five years ago inviting me here, I should have thrown it away, even though I didn't have five dollars to my name. I wish I had lived wildly instead. Anything—anything would have been better than this empty, wasted life! If I had been a wife, a mother, even a scandalous woman, at least I would have lived! Instead, I just existed, missing everything that life had to offer."

She stopped, then slowly walked to the wardrobe. She ripped out some soft white fabric from an old nun's gown. She fastened it to her head with Miss Webster's jeweled pins, like a veil.

For a long moment, she stared silently at her reflection. Her eyes were hollow, lost in thought.

Then, without another glance back, she left the house and walked down to the lake.

The next morning, the city built on the old ranchos told itself with a shiver that there had been a tragedy at Webster Lake.

But what truly happened—that deeper tragedy—no one ever knew.

The Tragedy of a Snob

I

The first twenty-three years of Andrew Webb's life were calm and steady, thanks to regular work, lots of exercise, and a healthy body. He lived in a small apartment in Harlem with his widowed mother and younger sister, Polly, who dreamed of becoming a teacher and showing that women could earn their own way in life.

At that time, Andrew made thirty dollars a week working as a bookkeeper at a large savings bank. His salary was enough to cover the family's expenses. When Andrew was sixteen, his father passed away, leaving behind less than two thousand dollars and their furnished apartment. Things looked tough for a while, but Andrew quit school and got a job. He was good with numbers, very steady, and little by little, he earned promotions and a better salary.

Andrew's Uncle Sandy, his mother's brother, lived alone on the old family farm in New Jersey. He lived like a miser, sending Mrs. Webb a ten-dollar bill every once in a while. She never asked him for help, thinking he was just as poor as they were. Twice a year, she visited him to clean up his house. Andrew and Polly hated these visits—they found their fat, messy, and talkative uncle hard to stand—but they were polite out of respect for their mother. Uncle Sandy always joined them for Christmas dinner, but his stingy gifts never made up for his bad manners at the table.

Even with their struggles, the little family was happy. Their apartment had worn-out carpets, faded furniture, and signs of strict budgeting everywhere, but there was plenty of love. Mrs. Webb was kind, strong, and healthy. Her face was faded, her black dress always a bit worn, but she carried herself like a lady who handled hard times with pride. Polly, cheerful and round-faced, looked just like her mother. Even with little money, she kept up with fashion by taking sewing classes and making her own clothes during the summer. She also helped keep her mother's wardrobe neat and stylish.

Mrs. Webb did most of the housework herself, with the help of a maid who came in during the day. There wasn't even space for a live-in helper.

Andrew was the star of the family. He supported them, stayed out of trouble, and kept a good attitude. They had never seen him lose his temper. The neighbors often heard about his proud habit of walking all the way home from his downtown office every evening, except Sundays and his vacations, as his mother always made sure to add. She believed in being exact.

The family also thought Andrew was very handsome. He was five feet ten inches tall, lean, and athletic-looking. His face was a little heavy and his head narrow, but he had no extra fat, and his skin was healthy and clean. Like Polly, he dressed nicely, even though he bought ready-made clothes. He had a good eye for picking the right ones.

When Andrew started to change, his mother and sister quietly worried he might be in love. But as time passed and no new woman entered their lives, they stopped worrying—and even stopped wondering. He wasn't quite the same Andrew anymore, but since he still gave generously, stayed good-tempered, and spent most evenings at home, they chose not to question him. He would sit with them while Polly or Mrs. Webb read aloud, and he never missed their nightly snack of beer, crackers, and cheese before bedtime.

II

One morning, while Webb was still happily living with his family, he read his usual copy of the Harlem edition of a New York newspaper during his long ride into the city. He went through the news, editorials, and special articles without feeling anything unusual. Just as he was about to fold up the paper, he noticed a long article about a fancy party thrown the night before by people named Webb. It was obvious they were very important because the article took up a lot of space, was published quickly instead of being saved for Sunday, and had big, impressive headlines.

Andrew read the article with a strange sense of personal interest. Without even realizing it, something inside him started to shift—his mind slowly began pulling away from the simple life he had always known.

After that, he made it a habit to check the Society pages to see what the Webb family was doing. His interest grew from there, and soon he was fascinated by the lives of all the rich and famous people. Before long, he was buying weekly Society magazines and the big Sunday newspapers, which his sister found amusing.

At first, the glitter and mystery of high society completely amazed him. It felt like stepping into a world of fairy tales, just like how stories of princes and princesses feel to kids. Even though Andrew was usually calm, practical, and not very imaginative, a small part of him craved beauty and excitement. In other people, that feeling might have turned into big dreams or a love for art. In Andrew's case, it grew into a stubborn kind of envy that people often call snobbery.

Little by little, Andrew began to feel angry at life. He thought it was unfair that he had been born into an ordinary family while others were born rich and powerful. He wished that, instead of being born on a New Jersey farm, he had been born into the wealthy Webb family living in a grand mansion on Fifth Avenue. Of course, Andrew didn't actually say it like that. If he had, it would've sounded more like, "Why couldn't I have been Schuyler Churchill Webb instead of just a nobody from Harlem? We're the same age. It could've just as easily been me."

Not long after he celebrated his twenty-third birthday with a cake made by his family, these thoughts started bothering him. By the time he turned twenty-five, they had completely taken over his mind. Still, he wasn't truly miserable—he was too healthy and had too good an appetite for that. But every week, he got more and more caught up in reading about the rich people of New York and Newport.

More often, especially during the busy season, he would stroll up and down Fifth Avenue between Forty-first Street and the Park, usually between four-thirty and five-thirty on nice afternoons. Those walks became the highlight of his day. He recognized most of the fashionable men and women just by looking at them. Even though he didn't know their names, he had seen them in the papers so often that he could guess who they were.

He became especially interested in the young women he saw. They were neat, confident, and dressed in simple but stylish outfits, with their hair done in a serious, tidy way. They looked nothing like the women he had grown up around, or the dreamy, old-fashioned beauties in his mother's favorite "Book of Beauty." To Andrew, these young women seemed almost like another species—not exactly human, though that wasn't really fair. As they walked quickly past him in their tailored dresses, with glowing cheeks and bright eyes, most people would probably have compared them to strong, well-bred racehorses.

Even though Andrew admired all the fashionable girls he saw, he especially liked the ones who moved with more grace than energy. When spring came and the Park turned green, he would stand in the plaza surrounded by tall hotels, the rumble of traffic behind him, and completely forget about the groups of girls, their little dogs, and the boys who tagged along. Ahead of him, the gates of the Park opened onto rolling hills that stretched almost all the way back to his home in Harlem. Right beyond the entrance was a curve in the driveway, and he never got tired of watching carriages come around the bend and head out onto the avenue. The bright, lively scene belonged to the stylish carriages, carrying elegant women who sat proudly, dressed in colorful outfits. The horses gleamed and danced, and parasols fluttered above their cheerful faces like butterflies. Andrew would stand there, amazed, feeling both thankful that he could witness something so beautiful and heartbroken that he wasn't a part of it.

When summer arrived and all of Society escaped to Newport—a place he half-believed was real—Andrew felt lonelier than the most bored clubman stuck in the city, too stubborn to go to Newport and too poor to travel to London. Then, about three years into his obsession, something unexpected happened. During his short summer vacation, while hiking through the woods, he met a group of people from the West who were very curious about New York. To Andrew, New York meant only one thing: high society, which he felt deeply connected to in his heart. Without realizing it, he started talking about New York's social world as if he lived right in the middle of it.

His careful, though limited, study of the rich and famous made him sound convincing to people who didn't know any better. He described the grand parties, the well-known people, and even copied the way Ward McAllister, a famous social figure, thought and spoke— something any newspaper reader might recognize. For a while, Andrew even fooled himself. He enjoyed pretending so much that he stayed with the curious group until his vacation ended. After that, every summer, he made sure to find another group of tourists to talk to about New York society—always slipping himself into the stories.

He wasn't exactly lying, at least not in the way most people think about it. At home and at work, he had a reputation for honesty. Like anyone else, he had his daydreams—he just chose to live his out loud in front of an audience. These summers became the happiest moments of his life.

Andrew had another special pleasure too. On the first day of every month, he treated himself to dinner at Delmonico's, a very fancy restaurant. At first, it meant giving up his usual cheap lunch, but he decided the experience was worth it. One evening, though, he stayed too long strolling along Fifth Avenue and arrived at the restaurant late. It was packed. He stood uncertainly at the door, knowing he couldn't sit at a table that was already taken, even if it was just one person.

Suddenly, a short, ordinary-looking man came up and tapped him on the arm.

"Hey, want to share my table?" the man said with a big, friendly smile. "I'm Slocum. I've seen you here a lot. Don't leave—come join me."

Grateful, Andrew agreed and followed Mr. Slocum to a small table across the room.

After Andrew ordered his meal, Slocum leaned in and said, "You know, I've had an idea for a while now. How often do you come here?"

"Once a month," Andrew replied.

"Same here!" said Slocum excitedly. "I'm just a clerk and don't make much money, but I have to have at least one good meal a month.

So here's my plan: why don't we share? One meal is enough for two, and we can split the cost. Makes sense, right?"

Andrew didn't really like Mr. Slocum—he was too plain and didn't fit in with the fancy crowd Andrew admired. But the offer was too good to pass up, so he agreed. For the next three years, until he turned twenty-eight, Andrew dined at Delmonico's every month, sharing meals with Mr. Slocum. Sitting in that elegant place, Andrew could almost forget about the small apartment he lived in back in Harlem. In those moments, he forgot he was Andrew Webb and imagined he really was Schuyler Churchill Webb.

III

One day, they got the news that "Uncle Sandy Armstrong" had died. Andrew couldn't leave work, and Polly, who was now a teacher, couldn't either. So their mother quickly packed an old carpetbag and went to handle her brother's funeral. That night, Andrew and Polly talked about their uncle's death in a very business-like way—something their mother would have found heartless, but which made sense to them.

"I guess Ma will get the farm," said Polly. She was still plump, rosy, and neatly dressed, though she now carried herself with more importance and spoke a little like a teacher. "How much do you think it's worth?"

Andrew, stretched out on the sofa with a pipe, pushed out his top lip and said, "About four thousand dollars—no more. The orchard's a mess, and the house is falling apart."

"We could mortgage the land and fix up the house for summer guests," Polly suggested, tapping a stack of student papers on the table next to her.

Andrew scowled deeply, but Polly didn't notice since she was busy daydreaming. Even if she had seen it, she wouldn't have understood why.

"May as well do that as anything else," he said, trying to sound casual. "Nobody's going to buy it, not with all that marshland."

Two days later, Andrew came home to find the whole place buzzing with excitement. Bridget, the kitchen maid, stood at the doorway at the end of the narrow hall, her face purple with excitement, her eyes shining.

"Oh, Mr. Webb!" she gasped, waving her arms wildly.

"Andrew, come here!" Polly screamed from the other end of the hall. "Come here, quick!"

Andrew usually moved slowly, but thinking something might be wrong with his mother, he rushed toward the parlor. There he found Mrs. Webb, sitting stiffly in a chair, looking a little shaky but healthy enough. She was holding a legal document on her lap. Polly was close to losing control, almost in hysterics.

"You'll never guess what happened!" Polly cried. "Tell him, Ma— I can't!" Then she threw herself face-down on the sofa and started kicking her heels in the air.

"We're rich, Andrew," said Mrs. Webb, struggling to stay calm. "Your Uncle Sandy had been investing wisely for the last twenty years. He left behind one hundred and fifty thousand dollars—fifty thousand for each of us."

Andrew's legs gave out and he dropped into a chair. Only one thought filled his mind. In a flash, the shabby little room disappeared from his imagination. He could finally have the life he had dreamed of for years.

"Say something, Andrew!" Polly shouted. "If you don't, I'm going to scream! Fifty thousand dollars all mine! No more teaching, no more dressmaking! We're going to Europe! Ma says it's invested so well that we'll each get four thousand dollars a year! Oh, goodness—oh, goodness!"

"I'd like to fix up the old house and live there," Mrs. Webb said thoughtfully. "But yes, I want to see Europe first. That was one of my dreams when I was young."

"And I'm finally going to get a sealskin coat!" Polly squealed. "And you'll get a beautiful black silk dress, Ma—and diamond earrings too—"

"Polly!" her mother interrupted. "What would I do with diamonds? A new black silk dress—something really nice—that's all I'd want. Poor Sandy!"

Andrew leaned forward, picked up the legal paper, and placed it on his knee. He ran his hand over it gently, almost like it was something precious. There wasn't much sentimentality in him, even though he admired beautiful things—especially the glamorous side of New York. After a while, he managed to join the conversation again. When they asked what he planned to do, he mumbled that he wasn't sure. But in truth, his plans were already very clear.

That night, he sat on the edge of his bed, staring at the old, faded rug with the picture of a boy and a dog under his feet. Fifty thousand dollars! It sounded like a huge fortune. Sure, he had seen numbers like that in bank records, but he had never thought of it as something real, like cash he could actually touch. Fifty thousand dollars! He didn't know exactly how much it cost to live like the wealthy people he admired. He just knew they lived easy, luxurious lives. And now, with his inheritance, he could finally join their world.

IV

The time between that night and the day the estate was finally settled felt like a restless dream for Andrew. Days, weeks, and months dragged on endlessly. He felt more disconnected than ever from his small world and completely lost in thoughts of the bright, exciting life he believed he was about to join. He didn't worry about how he would actually get into high society. To him, it seemed simple—as if the gates of Central Park, wide and open, welcomed anyone lucky enough to have money. The only thing that filled his mind was this: by July 1st, he would be free—free from his boring desk job, free to live the life he had dreamed of, free to go to Newport. Once he arrived there, he believed, everything would fall into place naturally.

At this point, Andrew still held onto a sense of pride. He felt he was just as good as the men he had seen at Delmonico's—the young guys with pink faces and fancy boots, and the friendly older men with big stomachs and puffy eyes. He had even picked up many of their little habits. Late at night, he would open the door between the kitchen and dining room so he had enough space, and practice the stylish walk of fashionable New York men: shoulders slightly hunched forward, body leaning a bit sideways, and a heavy, thoughtful step. The only real difference between their walk and that of the city's rougher crowd was the size of the steps. One hand stayed tucked into a pocket while the other casually twirled a walking stick. Andrew had also studied the proper handshake and felt confident he could do it just right.

On July 3rd, just an hour after the lawyers finished handing over the money, Andrew placed a huge order for a brand-new wardrobe from the most expensive tailor in New York. Those purchases and a few others took a big bite out of his first quarter's income, but he didn't care—he thought it was a small price to pay for the life he was about to live.

Meanwhile, his mother and sister were busy selling off the simple things from their apartment in an auction, getting ready for a year-long trip to Europe. They didn't really understand why Andrew was so determined to go to Newport, but they had heard it was a pretty town with a nice beach and popular with tourists.

Their last night together was spent in a hotel. Even though Andrew protested a little, Mrs. Webb insisted on ordering beer, crackers, and cheese for a small supper—just like they had done for years. The women were teary-eyed and wanted to make their final evening together feel as close to the old days as possible. It was a sad and bittersweet meal.

V

It was a brutally hot August day when Andrew stepped off the steamboat and finally set foot in Newport. Technically, he was standing on a wooden dock, and he wasn't very impressed at first. But as the stagecoach rumbled through town, his heart began to swell with excitement, and his usually dull eyes lit up. It was two o'clock in the afternoon, and the town was quiet, resting under blankets of ivy and flowers. After the constant noise of New York, the peace, the old-fashioned charm, and the elegance of Newport felt amazing. The clatter of the horses' hooves and the voices inside the coach seemed almost wrong in such a peaceful place. Through the trees, he caught glimpses of long, shady streets and grand homes hidden behind tall gates. To Andrew, it felt like he had entered paradise.

Even the hotel, simple and modest as it was, impressed him. It seemed old, calm, and highly respectable. Nervously, he got down from the coach and went into the lobby. A clerk handed him a pen, and Andrew neatly signed the register: "A. Armstrong Webb." He had decided to add his late uncle's name to sound more important. The clerk barely glanced at the name before handing him a key, and Andrew felt a small wave of disappointment. Still, he reasoned that even a nobleman traveling in secret would be treated the same way. He followed the bellboy upstairs to a plain room overlooking a small courtyard.

Feeling a little let down but trying to stay positive, Andrew went down to the dining room and was surprised to find that dinner, not lunch, was being served. He had expected fancy hotels in Newport to serve dinner at eight, not midday.

After eating, he settled onto a chair on the hotel's front porch, lit an expensive cigar, and tried to relax. But the loneliness quickly set in. There seemed to be almost no one at the hotel, and for the first time, he felt unsure. He had expected the hotel to be full of important people. Looking down the avenue, the huge houses hidden behind thick trees felt more like tombs than homes. Everything was just so still.

The cigar helped calm him a little, and he wandered back into the lobby where he struck up a conversation with the clerk, a cheerful little Englishman with rosy cheeks. The clerk immediately guessed that Andrew wasn't one of the fashionable crowd or a Newport regular, but he liked Andrew's honest look and was happy to chat. That's when Andrew learned the hard truth: the rich didn't stay at hotels anymore. If they had to for a few days, they stayed locked in their rooms. They lived in "cottages" now—huge, fancy homes they humbly called cottages. Most hotel guests didn't show up until the fifteenth, and even then, they were mostly tourists and older regulars who didn't bring much energy to the place.

Feeling more discouraged, Andrew left the hotel and wandered up the avenue. But as he walked under the thick, shady trees, his spirits lifted again. The avenue was so beautiful, so grand and quiet. He breathed in the rich, aristocratic atmosphere and felt its magic. His imagination ran wild. Leaning on a fancy iron gate, he pictured himself inside one of the stunning Queen Anne houses with its tall Tudor towers. He didn't care if the architectural styles clashed—it all seemed perfect to him. In his mind, he strolled through richly decorated halls, drank tea on the back veranda with elegant ladies and gentlemen, and lounged in armchairs while listening to a well-dressed girl play the piano. He imagined sitting beside a proud lady of the house, though he wasn't sure what they would talk about. Despite all the society novels he had read, he couldn't remember any real conversations. But he didn't care. In his daydreams, Newport belonged to him.

Back at the hotel porch, he lit another cigar and was about to plan his next move when something incredible happened. It was exactly four-thirty. Almost like the curtain had risen on a play, the once-empty Bellevue Avenue filled with life. Gates opened, and carriages rolled out in perfect timing, as if their owners were being paid to show up right on schedule. The avenue, bright with colorful dresses and fluttering parasols, looked like a giant spring garden.

Andrew forgot his cigar. He leaned forward, watching eagerly.

There were old ladies in fancy carriages, their heads nodding weakly, maybe wondering how much longer their money could keep them going. Some had young heirs riding beside them, patient and calm. Others sat alone. Horseback riders passed by, struggling to look fashionable while riding stiffly. Carriages filled with beautiful young women rolled past—girls with flawless ivory or rosy skin, looking delicate and perfect. Now and then, a dark carriage would pass by, carrying women dressed in heavy black veils, and Andrew wondered if they really grieved the same way ordinary people did.

Mixed in with the grand carriages were obvious rentals, carrying tourists trying a little too hard to look fancy. Every now and then, a local girl would ride by proudly on horseback, her jacket flapping open and a sailor hat perched on her head. Once, a girl even drove a pair of oxen right into the crowd.

Slowly, the avenue in front of the hotel emptied again. Farther up the road, a traffic jam of carriages had formed, all heading to the same place. Excited but unsure, Andrew rushed down the hotel steps, torn between following and staying put. A bunch of open carriages waited at the curb, and one of the drivers approached him.

"Want a ride, sir?" the man asked.

"Yes," Andrew said quickly. "Follow wherever the others are going."

"Sure thing," the driver said, grinning. "And if you're new here, I can tell you who's who."

Andrew almost tipped him right then and there. At last, he could finally start putting names to the faces he had dreamed about!

"We'll drive slow and meet them on their way back," the driver added. He pointed toward a passing carriage. "You see them, sir? Those folks just stay at the hotels and pretend they spent the summer in Newport. But anyone here can tell the difference. You can't fool the real crowd."

Andrew immediately understood. If he wanted to fit in, he couldn't keep staying at a hotel. He needed to rent a "cottage," just like the others.

They drove down a shady avenue and out toward the sandy hills by the sea. Mansions stood proudly on the high ground, looking just like the famous cottages Andrew had always imagined. He barely noticed the houses, though. His eyes were glued to the returning parade of carriages as the driver pointed out famous names—names that had sounded like music to Andrew for years. Some younger faces were new to him, but the names were familiar from all the newspapers he had read.

"Look sharp now!" the driver suddenly called out. "There's Mrs. Johnny Belhaven! She's worth more money than all the others put together—and she's one of the best carriage drivers in Newport!"

A plump but fancy-looking woman rode toward them in what looked like a grand chariot. Andrew had never seen anything so tall on wheels before. Mrs. Belhaven sat high up, looking down at everyone with a proud, almost unfriendly expression, like she was sitting on a throne.

"And there's Ward McAllister," the driver said excitedly. "He's the leader of the Four Hundred, you know."

Andrew almost jumped out of his seat. He stared wide-eyed at the tired-looking, carelessly dressed older man—the same man he had admired from afar for years.

When he got back to the hotel, Andrew felt much better. He had finally taken part in real Newport life. As he passed the lobby on his way to the elevator, the hotel clerk waved him over.

"Since you seem new around here," the clerk said politely, "I thought I'd introduce you to Mr. Chapman. He's a reporter for some New York papers. He can tell you how to enjoy yourself."

Mr. Chapman, a short, friendly man with a solid build, shook Andrew's hand warmly. He wasn't the type of person Andrew had dreamed of meeting, but Andrew was happy for the company.

They went out to the hotel's veranda, and Andrew offered him a cigar from his new case. Chapman accepted gratefully. He worked as a freelance reporter for a few New York weeklies and didn't earn much money. Leaning back in his chair and putting his feet on the railing, he confessed to Andrew that he hated Newport.

"I wouldn't have come at all this summer if I could've gotten out of it," Chapman said gloomily. "It's my third year, and it gets worse every time. The people here are so stuck-up that you can't get close enough to them for a story. Even Lancaster, who's connected to a big-name family, says it's almost impossible to get any information. He works for the New York Eye. And what's worse, they don't even do much. It's already August third, and there hasn't been a single real ball—just a few private things no one can get into. It's enough to drive a guy crazy. I've had to make up so many stories that my imagination's about worn out. But the papers have to get news somehow."

Chapman smiled proudly. "Still, I pulled off one big win this summer—a huge scoop. Did you see that new mansion halfway down the avenue with the stone wall around it? That's the new Belhaven place. They swore no reporter would ever get inside, no photos, nothing. The newspapers were desperate. Even Lancaster had no luck. I was determined to get in—even if I had to sneak in like a thief. But I didn't have to. I paid off their butcher to let me pretend to be his delivery boy. I hid a camera in the meat wagon, took pictures of the outside, and even flirted with the cook to sneak a look inside. The family wasn't up yet, so I dodged the butler and snapped a few more photos. The other reporters were furious, especially Lancaster. He had paid caterers and florists to give him the best stories first. That was a dirty trick—but honestly, I'd do the same if I had his paycheck."

Chapman leaned closer. "Last year, Lancaster got another big scoop. Mrs. Foster—she's a really big deal around here—redid her whole house. All the newspapers wanted photos, but she refused. Wouldn't even listen to Lancaster's begging. But Lancaster had bribed the butler. See, Mrs. Foster didn't live there full-time. She only visited every two weeks to rearrange the furniture. The poor butler was so stressed about keeping everything perfect that he bought a camera and photographed the rooms after every visit. He met Lancaster one day, told him about it, and of course Lancaster bought the photos. It cost the newspaper a fortune, but it was worth it. And Mrs. Foster never figured out how the papers got those pictures."

Andrew listened, feeling a mix of amusement and disappointment. He was beginning to understand just how closed-off and private the Newport elite really were—the same people he had come so eagerly to admire.

He quickly changed the subject.

"I don't want to stay here," he said, giving the hotel behind him a look of disgust. "What do you suggest? Should I rent a cottage?"

Chapman nearly choked. "Rent a cottage? Are you secretly a millionaire? Even if you were, I doubt you could get one. The rich folks either lock up their cottages when they're away or lend them to their friends. And the rest are taken by the same people every year."

Chapman thought for a second. "No, what you need is a bachelor's apartment. Those aren't easy to find either, but I happen to know about one. Jack Delancy rented it four years ago, but he lost most of his money and disappeared. The place is available now. We should go check it out right away—no time to waste."

Andrew quickly agreed, feeling deeply grateful he had met Mr. Chapman. The apartment was close to the hotel, still available, and had bold but tasteful furniture. The rent was steep, but Andrew pushed aside his worries about money and bravely wrote a check.

That night, there wasn't much happening in Newport—not even a moon in the sky. The town felt like a graveyard. With nothing else to do, Andrew spent the evening looking for servants. By the next day, he had moved in and even invited Chapman over for dinner to celebrate.

The next morning, Andrew found Chapman at the beach, snapping photos of the people swimming and sunbathing.

"This kind of thing sells," Chapman said, taking another photo. "Even though most of these people are just regular tourists, I label the pictures things like 'the beautiful Miss Brown' or 'the famous Miss Jones.' Readers eat it up, and the paper looks good. The real upper-class people won't mix with the crowd. They stay in their carriages over there, acting bored because they have nothing else to do. They wouldn't be caught dead sitting here like regular folks at Narragansett. They're too proud. Want to go up to the Casino and watch the coach leave? That's one of the main sights."

The night before, Andrew had spent a long time admiring the Casino building from a distance. Now he was excited to finally see some of its famous life up close.

They reached the Casino just a few minutes before the coach was set to depart. A large, round-shouldered man sat lazily on the coach, swinging his whip without much energy. A few girls, dressed in fancy versions of simple summer dresses and small hats, were already seated at the top. An older man was helping a young woman climb the ladder. She wasn't very pretty, but she looked healthy and wore a simple white dress.

"She's worth sixteen million dollars, all by herself," Chapman groaned.

On the sidewalk, between the Casino and the coach, two groups of girls gathered. One group cheered and chatted with their friends already on the coach, while the other group stood back, watching enviously. Andrew noticed a clear difference. The girls talking to the riders wore beautifully made organdie dresses, big Leghorn hats decorated with expensive flowers or feathers, and had a confident, polished air about them.

But the other girls—Andrew asked Chapman about them.

"Oh, they're locals," Chapman said. "We call them that to tell them apart from the summer people who rent the cottages. The locals try to copy the style and manners, but anyone can tell the difference."

Andrew felt a sudden pity he didn't want to admit. The local girls were pretty, with bright faces and second-rate clothes that reminded him of Polly's homemade outfits. The gap between the two groups was sharp and painful to see.

"I've got to run," said Chapman. "But I'll catch up with you later. Take care."

The horn sounded, the whip cracked, and the coach rolled away. The men watching from the club balcony barely stirred. Carriages blocking the road moved aside, clearing the way.

Andrew turned his attention back to the fashionable girls. One wore a bright yellow dress with black velvet ribbons and a big hat to match. She wasn't exactly beautiful, but she carried herself with such confidence that, to Andrew, she was stunning. Another wore lilac, another pink. They all had smooth brown hair and creamy skin. A tall, sleepy-looking young man with a huge mustache followed them, clearly trying to impress.

The group chatted for a while, then headed toward the Casino's grassy lawn and the lower balcony that wrapped around the building. Andrew, unable to resist, followed them. He copied the young man's lazy, stylish walk, climbed the steps, and casually took a seat across from the group, pretending not to notice them. He arranged his face into a blank, thoughtful expression, trying to fit in.

But it was a wasted effort. The girls acted like he didn't even exist. They only seemed aware of each other.

Andrew was shocked when one of the girls crossed her legs and swung her foot playfully. The young man slouched even deeper into his seat. Another girl arrived, and when she was introduced, he didn't even stand up or offer her a chair. She had to awkwardly pull one over by herself.

The band started playing, and Andrew leaned forward, pretending to study the ground while trying to hear what they were saying. But the music made it hard, and he only caught bits and pieces.

"My clothes keep disappearing," said the girl in yellow with a lazy drawl. "I think my maid wears them... I don't even know what I have anymore... I'm afraid to say anything."

Everyone laughed.

"Are you going to Paris this year?" someone asked.

"I don't know... I'll decide when the time comes. Then we'll keep four servants up all night packing. I'll need new gowns, of course... You have to talk to Ducet and Paquin yourself, you know."

The young man actually fell asleep, while the girls leaned in and whispered to each other. After a while, they got up with a flirty sort of air that completely enchanted Andrew—and wandered off across the lawn.

VI

That evening, while Andrew and Chapman sat drinking coffee in the fancy little dining room that once belonged to the unlucky cordage investor, Chapman suddenly said:

"I gotta say, buddy, you don't seem to fit in here. Don't you know anyone in Newport?"

Andrew shook his head, looking gloomy.

"Well," Chapman continued, "then you're going to have a pretty dull time. There are only three types of people who come to Newport—the rich folks, the people who come to watch the rich folks, and the reporters stuck here covering the rich folks. So, why exactly did you come?"

Andrew wasn't the type to open up easily, but a dark blush crept up his face. Chapman caught on right away.

"Too bad you didn't bring a few letters of introduction," Chapman said. "One or two would've made all the difference. You look the part, and you've got the money. Where are you from, anyway?"

"New York," Andrew answered.

Chapman whistled softly around his cigar. "That's rough. It's harder for a regular New Yorker to get into high society than for a lawyer to get into heaven. Didn't you have any fancy friends from college?"

"I never went to college," Andrew admitted.

"That's a shame," Chapman said. "College is the best place to make connections you can use for the rest of your life."

Bit by bit, using the skills that made him a good reporter, Chapman got Andrew to tell him about his life—and even about how much money he had. More than once, Chapman was shocked at Andrew's honesty and innocence, but he liked him too much to tell him outright that he didn't stand a chance. He figured it would be kinder to let Andrew realize it on his own, and then help him find a way out.

A few minutes later, Chapman stood up. "Well," he said cheerfully, "I wish I were someone important like Lancaster. Maybe I could help you then. But I'm not, not even close. You might as well go enjoy the sights anyway. The first big dance at the Casino is tonight. Get dressed up and go."

"Who's going to be there?" Andrew asked, trying to sound casual.

"Oh, all the cottagers, or most of them anyway. It's a beautiful scene."

"But how can I even get in?" Andrew asked.

"Easy," Chapman said, grinning. "Just pay a dollar at the door."

Andrew's cigar dropped from his mouth in shock.

"You mean to tell me," he said, "they just walk into a ballroom—and dance—in full evening dress—with anybody who pays a dollar to get in? Anybody?"

Chapman laughed. "Well, go see for yourself. Meet me in the gallery at ten. I'll point out who's who. See you later."

At half-past nine, Andrew stood in front of his mirror, studying himself carefully. Without being vain, he had to admit that he looked good. His strong, young build wore his tuxedo naturally, like a gentleman—not like a waiter. He had seen plenty of well-known men at Delmonico's who would've looked like staff without their fancy facial hair. Chapman had even pointed out two sons of important families whose thick sideburns made Andrew mistake them for coachmen.

He smoothed his own mustache. It was soft and silky, like the hair of the fashionable women he admired. His haircut was done by the most stylish barber in New York. He didn't wear jewelry, and everything about his appearance was neat and proper. He felt quietly proud. Still, under the surface, he felt a heavy sadness pressing on him.

The Casino was just a short walk from his apartment. He made it there without scuffing his shoes, bought a ticket—half expecting them to laugh in his face—and crossed the lawn to the main door. Inside, the ballroom was lit up brilliantly. With its open, elegant design, it looked like a place where fairies might throw a party. The cottagers, Andrew knew, entered through a different door since they were subscribers and didn't have to buy tickets.

He climbed up to the gallery to wait for Chapman. It was barely a quarter full, mostly with pretty girls—locals, Andrew realized right away. Some wore hats, and others were dressed up as best they could, in simple muslin or Indian silk dresses with flowers tucked into their hair.

Andrew took a seat at the railing. Next to him sat a striking dark-eyed girl who had clearly put a lot of effort into looking stylish. She wore a bright red silk dress and had a red rose in her thick hair. She had tied a piece of silk lace around her neck like a fancy choker.

Andrew, used to admiring the finest beauties, looked at her the way an art critic might glance at a colorful poster—not very impressed. But he was young, and so was she. They flirted a little, smiling and chatting, until Chapman showed up and introduced them properly.

"Miss Leslie is an old friend of mine, Webb," Chapman said warmly. "I hope you two get along."

Miss Leslie smiled brightly, showing off her perfect teeth, and gave a small, graceful nod. Andrew mumbled something polite, feeling like fate was making fun of him. But he quickly forgot about her when Chapman leaned in and whispered that the cottagers were arriving.

Andrew eagerly leaned over the railing. A group of plump older women and slim, graceful young girls were walking in. Some of the older ladies wore shiny white satin dresses covered in sparkling jewels. The young women, moving with a light, deer-like grace, had their shiny hair styled high like little walnuts on top of their heads. Their tiny waists and smooth, bare arms and necks kept Andrew's attention completely. Some looked pure and delicate in their white gowns, like Easter lilies, while others were as striking as rare orchids. One beautiful young woman, clearly married, wore a black gauze dress decorated with glittering stars and crescent moons along the neckline.

"Isn't she beautiful?" Miss Leslie whispered. "She married a French Duke. She was lucky—but she's so sweet she deserved it."

All the women wore very low-cut dresses.

"This feels a little like the old days when slaves were sold at the market around here," Chapman muttered.

A lively woman with dyed hair and worn clothes swept into the room with a strong, commanding presence, and people quickly gathered around her.

"Who's that?" Andrew asked sharply. "Her dress is dirty, her gloves are stained, and her hair's fake."

"Oh, she's a big deal," Chapman chuckled. "Sometimes even the important ones don't look perfect. She's going to be one of the leaders this season. Just watch." Then he pointed out more famous faces to Andrew.

The band started playing a waltz. Most of the men were older but still moved well as they danced with the girls. A few younger men worked hard to impress the wealthy older women. Watching, Andrew thought that the young women he admired danced awkwardly. Many of them were taller than their partners and looked like they might tip right over them. The shorter girls bounced around like little rubber balls. Groups of older women stood together chatting, and a large lady sparkling with diamonds sat at the center of one group. Chapman leaned closer and told Andrew she was a duchess.

"See that guy over there?" Chapman said suddenly, pointing with his pencil at a young man with a smug, empty look who was trying way too hard to act important. "A year ago, nobody cared about him. He was just some distant Webb relative. But then he got a lot of money, and now the family accepts him. He's a big shot now. It's a real shame you're not that kind of Webb. You look way more like a real gentleman than he does."

"Are any of the real Webbs here?" Andrew asked bitterly.

"Yeah, that old lady over there. She's like an ice chest," Chapman replied.

"And Schuyler Churchill Webb?" Andrew pushed, barely able to keep his voice steady.

"He just came in. He's talking to the French duchess."

Andrew stared across the room at the plain but confident young man. Somehow, even without great looks, Schuyler's natural charm and easy elegance hit Andrew hard, making him feel the gap between himself and the world he wanted more than ever before. What had seemed like a small distance before now felt like an impossible canyon.

"I've got to run," Chapman said. "Deadline's coming. See you tomorrow."

After Chapman left, Miss Leslie tried to start up a conversation again, hoping Andrew would invite her to dance. She was scared of the high-society crowd but felt safer with Andrew nearby. Still, Andrew quickly made an excuse and left. He had paid to be in that room, and he intended to make the most of it.

At the far end of the ballroom, three rows of chairs were clearly meant for people like him—outsiders. The cottagers filled the other three sides of the room, looking completely at ease, as if they owned the place.

Andrew walked confidently across the floor and claimed one of the empty seats. Only a few tourists like him sat nearby; most had gone upstairs to watch from a distance.

The room wasn't decorated, but the older women, glittering with jewels, formed a dazzling border around the dance floor, while the young women looked like a living garden full of colorful, blooming flowers.

VII

Andrew sat there for an hour, and by the end of it, he finally understood why the cottagers didn't care about the tickets being sold to outsiders. Not once did any of them glance coldly at the row of seats where he and the other tourists sat. Not once did they even seem curious about the few brave visitors who dared to step onto the dance floor.

It was as if Andrew and the others were invisible, like unwanted guests on another planet. The cottagers didn't say anything rude or do anything openly cruel—but they ignored the strangers completely, and that was enough to make them feel frozen out.

The cottagers behaved like one big, happy family. The young people were relaxed and cheerful with each other, as if they had grown up together. It was no wonder the outsiders felt so distant. During the "Lancers" dance, the cottagers nearly turned it into a playful game, laughing and moving around freely. It was like they were playing in the yard of one of their summer homes, while the strangers stood awkwardly outside the fence, watching.

To the cottagers, people like Andrew didn't exist at all.

At the end of the hour, Andrew stood up slowly, feeling heavy and tired. His face had gone pale, and his legs were shaky.

Now he understood everything.

***

Andrew's night wasn't over yet. As he walked down the passage behind the rows of chairs reserved for the cottagers, he spotted a girl who had just arrived. He froze, staring at her, wondering how he had ever thought other women were beautiful. If the women he had admired before were princesses, this one was a goddess. Only New York could have created someone with such a unique kind of beauty— different from the natural, graceful elegance of women from old European families. She was like a perfect, rare orchid, while they were like lilies from ancient gardens.

This girl was taller than most, with a slightly fuller figure that gave her a majestic look. She walked simply, yet it felt like she was used to walking among stars. Her shiny brown hair was twisted into a neat knot at the back of her classic-shaped head. Her forehead, chin, and throat were shaped so perfectly they looked sculpted. Her skin was so white and flawless it seemed to glow. You could probably examine it under a microscope and not find a single flaw. Her nose and mouth weren't perfectly shaped, but her large blue-gray eyes shone so brightly that none of that mattered, and her ears were delicate and beautiful.

She wore a simple, pale blue dress that hugged her figure perfectly, covering her neck and wrists. Beside her stood the new Webb relative—the same young man Chapman had pointed out earlier—half a head shorter and clearly not worthy of her attention. A few other men circled around her too.

Andrew didn't know if he was truly capable of deep love, but whatever love he could feel, he gave it to her immediately and completely. It was the kind of love philosophers like Schopenhauer and Darwin might have smiled at—pure, instinctive, and undeniable. But it wasn't romantic or passionate. He didn't see her as a person to love; he saw her as a prize, someone who would walk beside him at grand events, making others stare in envy. He loved the idea of what she represented more than the girl herself.

For a moment, his attention shifted when he noticed an old man putting on a ridiculous show in front of her. The man bowed, waved his hands, rolled his eyes, and acted like a fool trying to impress her. To Andrew, he looked like an old goat struggling with a thorn in its hoof. The girl looked down at him with good-natured amusement. The men around her laughed, and Andrew quickly locked his eyes back onto her, completely under her spell.

Suddenly, her clear, shining eyes met his. For a split second, Andrew felt a spark—but then she looked right past him with the indifference someone might show an empty space.

Andrew turned away, forgetting even his hat, and stumbled out of the ballroom, down the street, and up the stairs to his apartment. He dropped into a chair, buried his face in his hands, and let out a groan.

The full weight of his hopelessness crashed over him. He understood now: he had no chance at all. He might as well dream of flying to the stars as dream of entering the real world of New York society. There wasn't a single person on earth who could offer him a way in. Had he been some wild creature from a far-off land, he might have gotten more attention—at least for being exotic.

Behind the heavy curtains of his room, where no one could hear him, Andrew let himself cry. Tears ran down his face, and he twisted his strong hands together in pain.

Some might think his suffering was small compared to heartbreak, losing a child, or failing at a great dream. But anyone who truly understands human nature knows that the pain of a snob, trying and failing to belong, is real and sharp. An artist can work in obscurity and still find joy in creation. A politician can suffer defeat and still feel the pride of the fight. But a snob's struggle is constant humiliation—climbing endlessly toward something he can never truly reach, because the ones at the top were born there and never had to climb at all. For them, acceptance was automatic; for someone like Andrew, it was impossible.

And Andrew? He hadn't even taken the first step. For five years, he had lived inside a painful fantasy, and now it was gone.

He didn't even want the money he had anymore—it felt like a cruel joke. It couldn't buy the only thing he had ever wanted. His dream was shattered. He felt like an old man who had wasted his best years locked away, only to be released when it was too late to enjoy life.

As the sun rose over Newport, it shone kindly on the white yachts in the bay, on the grand old streets, on the rich history the cottagers ignored, and on the luxurious houses that made Newport famous.

And it slipped through a heavy pair of curtains, falling across the white face of a young man who had just learned that the world he longed for would never be his.

Crowned with One Crest

(Published in Vanity Fair, London, in 1895)

People were beginning to wonder if an American woman who had married into British nobility would ever give up her title for someone who was simply smart and good-looking. Specifically, they were curious if Lady Carnath—who had once been Miss Edith Ingoldsby from Washington, and before that, from Boone, Iowa, back when her father was just starting his rise to wealth and politics—would marry Butler Hedworth, a young politician with some money and a perfect family background, but no noble title.

So many American girls had quietly agreed to marry poor noblemen arranged by their mothers that, even when the English admitted these women were polished and well-mannered, they comforted themselves by believing that American girls didn't have real hearts.

Still, Lady Carnath, who had been a widow for only a year, allowed Butler Hedworth to show her open admiration. Quiet bets were being placed on whether she would end up marrying him. During her marriage to Lord Carnath, she had behaved perfectly, but one skeptic joked that women sometimes had very strange ideas—and the comment quickly spread.

The truth was, Edith Ingoldsby had paid a high price for her title, but she had honestly liked Lord Carnath more than almost any other man—except for one. When she married Carnath, she had been desperate to escape a powerful love that was tearing her apart.

At first, those old feelings stayed with her, but eventually, boredom and too much free time made them fade. She learned to enjoy her new life as an English countess. At first, it felt like she was living inside a storybook. But soon, her practical American instincts took over, and she realized it was just another chapter in the long story of her life. Her fortune, beauty, lively spirit, and her husband's title had put her among the highest ranks of society. If her heart had ever truly broken, it healed quickly without the pain of an unhappy marriage. When Lord Carnath died, she mourned him sincerely—but not so much that she wasn't eager for her mourning period to end. By the time she met Hedworth, her heart was as free and unburdened as if she had just stepped out of a convent.

"Yes, I was in love once," she told Hedworth one evening as they sat together. She blushed slightly as she stumbled over the word "before." Their relationship was still playful and full of unspoken tension—no one had made any official promises yet. "At least, I thought it was love. Every girl goes through those wild feelings when she's young. I had a few silly crushes when I was a teenager. But this one felt different—a real, serious love—probably because there was an obstacle. He was married. If he had been free, maybe it wouldn't have seemed so overwhelming. I was used to getting my way, and wanting something I couldn't have, combined with how magnetic he was, just made it worse. I let myself believe I was madly in love."

Hedworth stood up and leaned casually against the fireplace, looking down at her. They were sitting in her boudoir, a stunning yellow satin room that looked like the inside of a jewelry box. Lady Carnath's tall, elegant figure was outlined perfectly by her black chiffon gown. Diamonds sparkled on her neck, arms, and in her thick black hair. She had dressed for the opera that night but chose to spend the evening with Hedworth instead.

Her face was delicate but strong. Her lips were full and red, her eyes dreamy when she was calm, but lively and brilliant when she got excited. Her eyebrows were beautifully shaped, and her soft, dark hair, swept back from her low forehead, added to her graceful look. Hedworth studied her closely, as he had many times before.

"Well?" he asked, his voice quick and sharp, hinting at the temper and pride that many American women found charming in Englishmen. His face was finely shaped like most of his countrymen's, but his expressions were more lively. The strong set of his jaw and the athletic build of his body showed he was determined and tough.

"Well, what?" she said playfully.

"What kind of man was this Johnny?" Hedworth asked.

"I'm not very good at describing people," she replied. "He was very different from you—more easygoing, lighter in personality—"

"I don't care what he looked like," Hedworth cut in. "When a woman's in love, she sees a man the way she wants to. Was he in love with you?"

"Yes, of course he was," she said.

"Did he ever tell you?"

Lady Carnath's face turned a deeper shade of red. "Yes, he did."

"And you told him you loved him too?"

"Yes," she said quietly.

"What happened after that?"

"You're getting very curious," she said with a teasing smile. "But you don't need to know everything."

"You don't have to answer if you don't want to," Hedworth said. "But—did he kiss you?"

"Yes," she said proudly, lifting her chin. "We had a big, emotional scene. I probably bored him to death with all my drama."

"And he stayed calm through it all?" Hedworth asked.

"Yes. He was completely calm," she answered.

"Where did this happen?" he asked next.

"In the drawing-room," she said. "One afternoon after he walked me home from a tea party."

"What happened the next time you saw him?" Hedworth asked.

"I never saw him alone again," she said quietly.

Hedworth's face softened, and when he spoke again, his voice was much gentler. "Why not?"

She sat up straighter and answered boldly, "Because I didn't dare. Soon after that, Lord Carnath came into my life, and I accepted his proposal. Why are you smiling like that? One choice was just as bad as the other. But at least the path I chose didn't create a scandal."

"Exactly," he said. "All the gossip, rude comments, and nasty rumors—whether in the papers or whispered behind your back— would have worn you out. How do you feel about him now? If he were free and came back to you, would you marry him?"

She shook her head, looking up at him with a smile and another blush. "He's no more important to me now than the storybook heroes I used to think I was in love with."

"Why didn't he just get a divorce and marry you? I thought getting divorced was easy in America," Hedworth asked.

"You English think you know everything about America," she said, laughing softly. "You'll believe anything but never bother to really learn. Honestly, it seems like your pride would be hurt if you knew as much about America as we know about Europe. You act like old people hearing about some new invention—they don't understand it, so they pretend it's not worth knowing."

He smiled, like he always did whenever she got fired up about her country. "You still haven't answered my question."

"What was it again? Oh, divorce," she said. "If a man has a decent wife, even if they don't get along, he can't just leave her unless he's cruel—and I wasn't about to fall for that kind of man."

"'Like' him?" Hedworth asked, raising an eyebrow. "I thought you said you loved him."

"I don't think it was real love," she said. "I explained that already."

"Then why did you change your mind?" he asked.

"I've never met a man who asks so many questions," she said, teasing him.

But before the night ended, Hedworth had gotten all the answers he wanted.

***

Edith was excited thinking about how much attention her engagement would get, but she decided not to announce it right away. She liked the idea of keeping her happiness private for a little while, and she also felt she owed some quiet respect to Carnath's memory. She was truly happy—happier than she thought she could ever be again. She had once believed that after your first real love, your heart stayed buried, like the dead, until something brought it back to life.

Hedworth had taken her love without asking, and even though he could be jealous and demanding, Edith, knowing how changeable men could be, decided to be smart about keeping his attention. She found she could show many different sides of herself, like colors shifting in a kaleidoscope. When Hedworth needed peace, she stayed calm, but most of the time she kept him interested by changing her moods in clever ways. Maybe it made her even more attractive to him, but the truth was she didn't need to try that hard—he was already deeply in love with her. Still, he worried something might go wrong before she agreed to set a wedding date.

Both of them were too practical to stay trapped in worry for long. Whenever doubts crept in, they laughed them off and stayed happy when they were together.

Luckily, Edith was the kind of woman who was happy to give everything in love without expecting more than what a man could realistically offer. She was content being loved, wanted, and admired. Even though Hedworth's pride sometimes made him demand all her understanding without offering much in return—caring mostly that she was perfect in his eyes—she accepted it. She was smart, but not so clever that she overcomplicated things. Their chances for a good marriage looked strong.

But then something strange happened.

Hedworth had to leave for Switzerland because his mother became sick. Their goodbye stretched for hours, and for a few days afterward, Edith told herself she was heartbroken. But Hedworth's letters came often, full of energy and affection, and soon Edith found herself enjoying this new part of their relationship—waiting eagerly for the mail, feeling excited when she spotted his letter at breakfast, and imagining what he was doing from the little pieces he shared.

With the busy social season over, Edith stayed in town with not much else to do but wait for him to come back.

One hot night, sitting alone in her bedroom with the windows wide open, she began thinking deeply about Hedworth. She stared out over the dark tree-tops of the Park, tracing back every step of how her feelings for him had grown.

Then, all at once, a strange thought hit her—it all felt eerily like her first real love. Curious, and unable to resist digging into her own heart, she went back to those old memories. To her surprise, they weren't painful. They felt vivid and fresh, like they had been waiting quietly for her all along.

She relived it all: the first spark of interest, the excitement when he was near, the jealousy when he wasn't, the shock of realizing she had fallen into a love she never thought possible. She remembered how thrilling—and frightening—it had been, how sweet the danger felt.

There had been weeks of quiet friendship before he confessed his feelings. Looking back now, she realized he had handled everything with calm, expert care—someone who knew women very well but didn't lose control easily, even when he clearly cared.

She smiled a little, remembering how she had wanted to "save" him—to pull him away from his faults and help him grow into something better. She remembered the long nights when she had paced the floor, too miserable to eat or sleep, even pounding the walls in frustration.

The memories felt shockingly fresh. Even the happiest moments, which usually fade first, came rushing back clearly.

She got up and walked around the room, feeling amused but also unsettled.

"What does this mean?" she wondered. "Is there some invisible soul out there made for me, and pieces of it are in different men? Does the man with the biggest piece win my heart? Is that why people can fall in love more than once? Because this feels so much the same— almost ridiculously so."

She tried to think about Hedworth, but her mind kept drifting back to the first man. She half-expected to see his ghost standing in the dark window. His memory was so strong that she felt like she was living those old days all over again.

She thought about how much he had suffered and how she had always wanted to comfort him. That old sympathy and tenderness came rushing back.

She wondered where he was now, what he was doing. She didn't think he had loved another woman after her—he had nearly used up all his ability to love when he loved her.

And yet, she also knew, without a doubt, that if both men stood in front of her right now, she would choose Hedworth.

Still, whenever she pictured Hedworth in her mind, the shadow of the first man was always there too—standing behind him, watching with that half-sad, half-cynical smile he had worn the day he finally confessed he loved her.

"Is it the old love asking for its place again, not the man himself?" she wondered. "Is it true that what women really want is just to be loved, and that it doesn't matter whose arms it comes from, as long as they're attractive? Do I love Hedworth—or just the feeling he gives me? Now that I even question this, can I still be happy? Will that ghost always be there, looking over his shoulder?"

Edith was practical and sensible. She wasn't about to let her imagination ruin her future. She pressed the button for the maid and quickly wrote a letter to her old love—a simple, friendly note without anything emotional, just asking how he was. She figured that seeing his handwriting again—and whatever he wrote back—would help her finally figure out how she really felt. And maybe he was dead. Maybe it was his spirit that had been stirring up her imagination. She wasn't a superstitious woman, but she was smart enough to admit she didn't know everything—and not to completely dismiss anything, either.

Hedworth didn't come back for three weeks. During that time, it felt like her mind had turned into a battlefield where the two men were constantly fighting. Whenever she thought of one, the image of the other popped up too.

When she thought about Hedworth, she realized he was just playing the same familiar notes in her heart that had been awakened long ago. But for the first man—the one who had struck those notes first—she still felt a deep, stubborn tenderness. As the days dragged on, she waited anxiously for a letter from him.

Yet even as she thought about him, she didn't want to see him again. She only wanted Hedworth—and her longing for him grew stronger every day.

Then Hedworth returned—and the other man's memory disappeared.

***

Edith finally announced her engagement. She and Hedworth had been invited to many of the same houses for the fall season. Because there were so many social events, they hardly got any time alone. They had to sneak away into quiet rooms or take walks in the woods just to talk. At first, it was exciting. But when they ended up at a huge house party where it seemed like every space was packed with people, and two days passed without even a short conversation, Hedworth decided he had had enough.

He found her alone for a moment and said firmly, "Four weeks from today, we're getting married."

Edith gave a little gasp but didn't argue.

"I'm tired of all this waiting and talking," he said. "We'll get married at your house in Sussex on October second."

"Very well," Edith agreed calmly.

After that, Edith traveled to Paris to meet with designers who could make her look even more beautiful. Then she visited Hedworth's mother in Switzerland. Hedworth joined her there, but they spent so much time together that his poor mother barely saw them. Edith returned to England alone. Hedworth planned to follow her a few days later and stay with a friend whose estate was right next to Edith's.

A few days after she got back, Edith was sitting at her dressing table when a letter arrived, marked from Washington. Her maid was trying out a new hairstyle on her, but Edith wasn't happy with it. She quickly glanced at the envelope, recognized the handwriting, and set it aside. She told the maid to fix her hair in the simple way she preferred. Once the final pin was in place, Edith checked her reflection in the mirror, slipped out of her house shoes, and tried on a pair of new slippers from Paris—she was expecting guests for tea.

Then she remembered the letter and opened it:

Dear Lady Carnath—

I spent the whole summer in Canada, and no one forwarded my mail. I just found your letter here at the Metropolitan. Thank you for writing. I'm doing well. Nothing much has changed—I eat, drink, and slowly grow older. But you are still a memory I'm thankful for, and I've never tried to forget you. I was happy to hear from Tower, who I ran into in Montreal, that you are doing well and are happy. I hope that never changes.

There were several more pages with news about old friends and updates from home.

"Poor fellow," Edith thought with a sigh. "But honestly, I don't think any woman or any situation could ever make a man like him truly happy. And here I am, not even dressed yet for my guests!"

Still, even after she got dressed and went about her day, thoughts of her old love stayed in her mind, quietly pushing Hedworth to the background. Since Hedworth was still delayed in Switzerland, the memory had room to grow.

She didn't answer the letter right away. It was hard to know what to say. But the letter stayed in her mind, pressing on her, until she finally sat down at her desk with a pen, staring into space.

As she sat there, the memory of her first love completely took over her thoughts. Her face grew pale. It hit her hard: if this old love refused to leave her heart, maybe she had no right to marry Hedworth. If the ghost of her first love stayed with her after marriage, would she feel like she was betraying her husband?

Carnath, her late husband, didn't even enter her mind. His memory felt like just a small, unimportant part of her life.

She was sure she didn't want to actually see the first man again. She knew that if she did, whatever power he had over her would disappear. He was part of the past—and in her busy, lively life, the past didn't stand a chance.

"Is it really him that I miss?" she wondered. "Or is it everything he made me feel, everything he woke up inside me? Maybe the soul only falls in love once. Maybe even if the body and mind move on, the soul stays tied to the first person it chose. Maybe when women marry someone they don't love deeply, their soul just falls asleep. But when the right person comes along, the soul wakes up, lonely and desperate."

She bit hard on her pen. "Has any woman ever been in such a mess before? It feels so unreal, but at the same time, painfully real. Should I send Hedworth away and spend my life haunted by memories? Some women can survive on memories, but I can't. If I let Hedworth go, would the memory of the first man fade too? Maybe real passion is the only thing that wakes the soul. Until Hedworth made me feel fully alive again, I hadn't even thought about the first man—not even during my mourning year, when I was mostly just bored. What should I do? I can't throw away my life. I'm not a foolish, gloomy person. But I also can't marry Hedworth if what I feel for him is just the shadow of something I once felt for someone else. If this were a novel, Hedworth would suddenly get sick and die, and everything would sort itself out."

Her face went even whiter as another truth hit her: no woman could ever suffer the same way twice. That deep, soul-crushing heartbreak she had once felt belonged completely to the first man. Her heart could never break that badly again. If Hedworth left her or died, she would miss him, she would mourn him—but she would never feel that kind of pain again. Her first love had used up that part of her forever.

She sat there, heart pounding, thinking, "What should I do? What should I do?"

She dipped her pen into the ink and began to write a polite, distant reply to the man from her past—something sympathetic but careful, knowing it wouldn't change anything between them.

Then she heard footsteps on the gravel path below her open window. She jumped to her feet, her heart racing. She ran to the window and leaned out, smiling and trembling.

Hedworth was standing there, looking up at her, his eyes bright and full of life.

In that moment, it was clear. Edith belonged to the lively, complicated world around her—not the lonely, quiet world of memories and regrets.

Death and the Woman

(This story first appeared in Vanity Fair, London, in 1892)

Her husband was dying, and she was alone by his side. The room around them felt painfully empty and silent. They were in a small, stuffy room on the third floor of a New York boarding house. It was summer, and most of the other guests had gone away to the countryside. All the servants had been dismissed except for the cook, who spent most of her time sleeping upstairs on the fifth floor. Even the landlady had gone away for a short holiday.

The window was open to let in the heavy, unmoving air. No sounds came from the long, narrow yards or the tall houses nearby. The buildings muffled the usual noise from the streets. Every so often, the elevated train rumbled by in the distance, its grunts and squeals softened by the thick, hot air.

She sat there, overwhelmed by the deepest kind of grief—the kind that has no hope left. She stared blankly at the man lying there, breathing faintly. He had been her friend, her companion, and her lover for five years. Even though their lives hadn't been easy, their youth and hope had kept them strong. Now his body was thin and worn from illness. His face was hollow, and his nightshirt hung loosely on his once-strong frame. She was almost relieved that his body had changed, that the beauty she had loved had moved somewhere beyond the reach of death.

She had loved his hands especially—their strength, their warmth. Now they lay limp and yellow on the blanket. She knew they were already cold and starting to sweat. For a moment, a wave of pain shook her. They were gone too. She whispered the word to herself, then added "forever," as the memory of his touch rushed back to her.

Suddenly, she leaned over him. He had to still be there somewhere. If he was still breathing, then the soul, the true person inside him, hadn't left yet. Why couldn't she feel him? Was he trapped inside the dying body, still conscious, unable to break free? Was he suffering, seeing her heartbreak, wishing it would end? She called his name and even shook him gently, desperate to somehow reach him. But even in her madness, she knew that any roughness might send him away faster.

He didn't respond. She opened his gown and pressed her cheek against his chest, calling him again. Their bond had always been so deep, so real. How could he be gone if she still felt so connected to him? Until his body stopped breathing, he had to be there, didn't he? She couldn't understand how he could seem as distant as if he were already in his grave. But even with her cheek on his chest, the faint beat of his heart didn't change.

She waved her hands wildly in the air above him, grabbing at nothing, as if she could catch his soul before it slipped away. Then, feeling a surge of panic, she ran to the window. She was terrified she might lose control and scream for help. She had insisted on being alone with him for these final hours. She didn't want to lose her mind now.

She looked out and noticed she couldn't see the green grass in the yards anymore. A heavy darkness seemed to cover everything. She realized that night had fallen.

She hurried back to the bed, heart pounding, scared that she had been away too long and he might have died. His face was still visible, still frozen in the same expression. She pressed her face to his, but recoiled in horror. His skin was already cold, and she shivered violently.

She collapsed into her chair, pressing her hands against her chest. She stared at him with wide, frightened eyes as his face began to fade into the darkness. She didn't dare light the gas lamp; it would attract mosquitoes, and she didn't want to close the window and take away even the little bit of air left for him. Besides, she didn't want to see the terrible moment when his eyes opened for the last time or his jaw dropped.

Her vision became so strained that eventually everything blurred. She closed her eyes, waiting for tears to come and relieve the pressure. When she opened them again, she could no longer see his face. Thick clouds had covered the stars. It was completely night now.

Carefully, she leaned down and put her ear to his mouth. He was still breathing. She almost kissed him, but then pulled back sharply, heartbroken. These were not the lips she had loved. She couldn't accept anything less.

His breathing was so faint that sitting back in her chair, she couldn't hear it at all. She realized she might not even notice the exact moment he died. Determined not to fail him, she stretched out her hand and placed it firmly over his heart. Their bond had always been strong, and now, she owed it to him to stay with him until the very end.

She sat there in the hot, heavy night, pressing her hand firmly against her husband's fading heartbeat, waiting for Death to come. Suddenly, a strange thought crossed her mind. Where was Death? Why was he taking so long? Who was keeping him away? Which way would he come from? It felt like he was moving toward her with slow, steady steps, like soldiers marching to a funeral.

Her mind wandered. She thought of the slow, dramatic music that always played in theaters right before something important happened. She had always thought that was silly—and so had he.

She shook herself angrily for letting her mind drift and pressed her hand harder against his chest. Sweat broke out on her face. Then she let out a shaky breath. He was still alive.

But again, her thoughts drifted. Death—where was he? It was so strange to be alone in this big, empty house—she knew the cook had snuck out—waiting for Death to come and take her husband away. No, Death wouldn't burst in. He would creep silently, like evil sneaking up on innocence. Death was sneaky and unfair, and there was no way to fight back. If only Death would come openly, like a man, she thought bitterly. Even women had managed to fight giants when they had a weapon. But against Death, there was no weapon.

Suddenly she gasped in horror. Something was crawling over the windowsill. Her whole body froze, but somehow she managed to stand up and turn around, even though it felt like her eyes were moving against her will. Two small green lights glared at her from the window—then a cat jumped down, and the lights disappeared.

She realized how badly she was shaking. "Am I really this afraid?" she thought. "I always thought I was brave. He used to call me brave. But then, with him, it was easy not to be scared. And I begged them to leave me alone with him as my last wish. How shameful!"

Even though she was still trembling, she sat back down and pressed her hand to his heart again. She wished she had asked someone to stay just outside the door. There was no bell in the room, and she couldn't scream for help. That would feel like she was disrespecting him—and she couldn't bear to leave him, even for a moment. To come back and find him dead, to know he had died alone, was unthinkable.

Her knees knocked together. She couldn't deny it anymore—she was terrified. Her eyes darted around the room, wondering if she would actually see Death when he came. How close was he now? Not far, she thought. Her husband's heartbeat was so faint.

She remembered hearing that even brave people could be driven mad by the sight of a corpse. She had never been scared of the dead before. But this—waiting for Death to come—was different. And she might be waiting for hours, through the dead of night, while something terrible crept closer and closer.

She bent over her husband in anger and despair. Where was the strong spirit that had always protected her? How could he leave her like this? How could he abandon her? She leaned back in the chair, her head moving restlessly against the cushion, groaning in grief. She pictured him as he used to be—and then the fear came back, freezing her once again.

Suddenly, she heard something—a faint, careful sound far below, like someone creeping up the stairs. Each step seemed to take forever, as if the person was trying hard not to be heard. She gave a shaky gasp. "Where's the slow music now?" she thought wildly.

Her face and body were soaked with sweat, and she felt a strange tightness at her scalp, as if her hair were standing on end. She couldn't lift her hand to check; her muscles were useless, her nerves twitching helplessly.

She knew it wasn't her ears—it was something deeper inside her, something that sensed Death moving through the house. Death was climbing the stairs, slowly, like an old, tired man. But how could he take his time when so many people were waiting for him? Maybe he had helpers for the less important deaths, but for moments like this, he came himself.

She could hear him reach the first landing, then shuffle quietly down the hall to the next set of stairs. Then he started climbing again, step by slow step. The footsteps were light, but steady and sure. They didn't pause, didn't turn back.

Her hand shook as she pressed it harder against her husband's heart. The beats were almost gone. She had a terrible thought: his heart would probably stop exactly when those footsteps reached the bed.

She wasn't even a person anymore. She was just a mind and an ear, listening to the terrible sound inside the silent house. Not even the distant elevated trains made any noise now—only those slow, relentless steps.

She found herself counting the steps aloud, irritated by how long it took between each one. The footsteps grew louder and heavier, crashing on the stairs like iron boots. She realized she didn't even need to know how many steps there were—the sound alone told her Death was almost at her door.

She heard the footsteps turn the corner and move down the hall toward her. They stopped right outside her door. Then heavy iron knuckles knocked hard on the thin panels. She couldn't speak, couldn't invite whoever—or whatever—was outside to come in.

The knocking grew louder, more demanding. The walls seemed to shake. The doorknob turned firmly and swiftly.

In a wild, desperate movement, she threw herself into her dying husband's arms.

***

When Mary opened the door and walked into the room, she saw a woman lying lifeless across the body of a dead man.

A Prologue

(TO AN UNWRITTEN PLAY)

Characters: James Hamilton, Mary Fawcett, Rachael Lavine, two slaves

Place: Nevis, British West Indies

Time: April, 1756

[A large, simple room with wide open windows. Heavy wooden shutters with iron bars are attached to each one. Outside, tropical trees with bright flowers and noisy birds and monkeys fill the view. In the courtyard below, there's a fountain. Between the trees, the blue of the sea can be glimpsed. The house sits halfway up a mountain. Inside, the room is plain—no curtains, no carpets, no soft furniture. But there are two polished mahogany pieces, a bookcase filled with old leather-bound books, a table with tropical fruits and pitchers of cool drinks, some potted palms, and Caribbean pottery on shelves. A harp stands quietly in one corner.

In the distance, a deep, rumbling sound grows louder. Dark clouds rush across the sky, and everything is covered in a strange, pale light.

Mistress Fawcett stands by a window, leaning on her crutch, listening carefully. Two slaves crouch fearfully on the floor. Suddenly, the sharp boom of four cannon shots echoes one after another. The slaves scream and press themselves even closer to the ground, as if trying to hide. Mistress Fawcett quickly slams the window shut, pulls the heavy shutters closed, and bars them. Down the hall, the sound of other windows being shut and locked thunders through the house. Mistress Fawcett tries to close another window, but it's stuck, and she isn't strong enough.]

MISTRESS FAWCETT (to the slaves): Come here! Close this window! Didn't you hear the cannons? A hurricane is coming!

THE SLAVES (still crouching, barely understandable): Oh, mistress, save us! Call the obeah doctor!

MISTRESS FAWCETT: Bring in one of those fools who promise magic? They're probably already hiding underground. Only our own strength and courage can save us today! (She bangs her crutch hard on the floor.) A hundred strong men on this estate, and not one to help? Is it up to my daughter and me to do everything? Get up!

THE SLAVES (whimpering, not moving): Oh, mistress!

[Enter RACHAEL. She walks calmly to the open window and looks outside.]

MISTRESS FAWCETT: Close the window, Rachael. I can't. These two are useless.

RACHAEL: In a minute.

MISTRESS FAWCETT: In a minute? Are you waiting for the roof to blow off?

RACHAEL: The hurricane is still a long way off.

MISTRESS FAWCETT: Dear God! How can you just stand there? In an hour, if this house isn't strong enough, we could be swept into the sea! These cursed Caribbean islands have tested my courage before, and I'll face this storm without flinching—but I can't stand seeing you so calm.

RACHAEL: Do I really seem calm? (She closes and locks the window.) It's a powerful sight. We might never see anything like it again.

MISTRESS FAWCETT: And we might not survive it either.

RACHAEL (with her back still turned as she secures the window): And if we don't, what does it matter? Are you so in love with life?

MISTRESS FAWCETT: Even at sixty, I'm not ready to be blown out of it. And if I were twenty—

RACHAEL (whirling around to face her): If you were twenty, with forty long years of emptiness ahead, trapped on this little island, what then? (She snaps her fingers.) That's what I think of the worst a hurricane can do!

MISTRESS FAWCETT (uneasy): Let's not talk about personal matters today.

RACHAEL: I've never felt more personal in my life.

MISTRESS FAWCETT (studying her carefully): I think you're excited.

RACHAEL (clenching her fists and pressing them to her chest): Excited? Call it what you like. All my life, I've been waiting for a hurricane—and now it feels like it's coming straight for me.

MISTRESS FAWCETT (trying to change the subject): I don't always understand you, Rachael. You're such a strange girl.

RACHAEL (suddenly letting her real feelings show): Strange? Just because I want to feel the mountain shake the same way my whole life has been shaken these past terrible weeks? Because I want to hear the wind roar and scream, breaking down human pride and showing us how small and helpless we really are?

MISTRESS FAWCETT: Hush! What are you saying? I can barely recognize you—you used to be as calm and still as a frozen flower! The storm must have gotten into your head.

RACHAEL: I'm not denying that. (She laughs.) But I won't lie—this is the real me. Whether you believe it or not, I'm finally showing who I really am. Which Rachael did you think you knew? First, I was the girl who loved books, the sunshine, the sea, and dreams of a future no man could control. Then, just when I was barely old enough to put my hair up, you forced me to marry a cruel man. After a year of silent suffering, I ran away from him in the middle of the night—back to you, the only person I had left to trust.

MISTRESS FAWCETT: Not another word! I trusted him! Every mother on St. Kitts was jealous of me! No one could have guessed—

RACHAEL: No one except a sixteen-year-old girl that no one would listen to.

MISTRESS FAWCETT: I told you to be quiet.

RACHAEL: Then order the hurricane to be silent too! I will speak!

MISTRESS FAWCETT: Very well. Speak. It might be our last chance anyway. (She sits down firmly, gripping her crutch tightly.)

RACHAEL: Did you really think you knew me during those two years when I barely spoke? When I hid in the shadows, scared of every man's voice? Later, my health returned, and I found new things to care about—but not hope. Never hope. By the time I was nineteen, I felt older than you do at sixty! And then—four weeks ago—

MISTRESS FAWCETT: Ah!

RACHAEL: Then James Hamilton came—and everything changed. I never thought I could look at another man without fear or disgust. Maybe true wisdom lies somewhere between being young and being old. But the law still ties me to a man who doesn't deserve to live. When I met Hamilton, something inside me woke up. For the first time, I wanted children. I saw goodness in people. Life suddenly seemed wide open and full of excitement, too big to ever be finished. And if I dare love the man who made me feel alive and strong, my husband could still ruin and disgrace me!

These past four weeks have been a crazy mix of happiness and heartbreak—and all the while, I had to pretend to the world that I didn't feel anything at all! Can you really blame me for welcoming this storm? During a hurricane, all people care about is surviving. In all this chaos, I finally feel free—alive—strong—just like the wild wind outside! I'm ready to tear down walls, to fight, to win, to live—live—live! Why should I care about what the world calls civilization? If James Hamilton called out to me right now from the middle of the flying trees, I would run to him without even thinking.

Listen! Do you hear it? Isn't it amazing?

[The hurricane is almost right on top of them. The deep roaring is mixed with sudden blasts of wind, crashing waves, the screams of frightened people and animals, and the wild clanging of church bells. From downstairs, there's the sound of people running, windows slamming shut, and hurried, nervous voices.]

MISTRESS FAWCETT: The slaves have all run into the cellar—every single one, probably more than two hundred! God help them, or they'll die down there from fear or lack of air. There's no hope of bringing them back up now. Even these two here are just waiting for a chance to run. Look!

[The slaves crawl toward the door on the left. Their faces are pale with fear, and they are gasping for breath. Rachael quickly runs over, grabs them by their long hair, and gives them a rough shaking.]

RACHAEL: Wake up! Wake up! We need your help! We have to keep an eye on the windows every moment!

[A powerful gust of wind rocks the house. As soon as Rachael lets go, the slaves collapse again, grabbing onto her skirts and crying softly. Rachael looks at them for a moment, lifts her foot like she might kick them, then shrugs and opens the door.]

RACHAEL: Go, then. Die however you want. Maybe someday I'll have the same right.

[The slaves stumble out.]

MISTRESS FAWCETT: I see you're following only your own will tonight. Those slaves are mine, and I told them to stay. But they were no help anyway. As for you—enjoy your moment of freedom. I made enough people bitter in my time. Maybe this is your last night too. And—thank God—Hamilton isn't here.

RACHAEL (suddenly alarmed): Where is he? Is he out at sea? Trying to cross the mountain with nowhere to hide?

MISTRESS FAWCETT: Trust a man, especially a Scot, to take care of himself. He's probably over on St. Kitts, drinking swizzle with Will Hamilton. Will's house is one of the strongest on the islands. Look!

[A powerful gust blows one of the shutters open, breaking the outer window. Leaves and shards of glass fly into the room. Rachael and Mistress Fawcett rush to the heavy wooden shutter and, using all their strength, manage to bolt it closed again. Then they move to check the other window. Mistress Fawcett sinks into a chair, gasping for breath and clutching her chest.]

RACHAEL: I'll go check the other windows! (She runs out quickly.)

MISTRESS FAWCETT: If only she knew! Hamilton was here on Nevis just an hour before the warning guns fired. I wouldn't be surprised if he helped fire them, since he's staying at the Fort. If I hadn't forced him to leave this afternoon, he would be here now.

Thank heaven—no man could survive a storm like this! I know Rachael better than she realizes. Will she still obey me after I'm gone? No! (She presses her hand harder against her heart, trying to stay calm.)

[Rachael comes back. She pours a drink and makes her mother take it. Rachael lifts her head, straining to listen. Her nostrils flare, and she seems to be catching every tiny sound. The roar of the wind grows louder. Now they can hear a rattling sound—the seeds shaking in the dry pods of the giant tree.]

RACHAEL: Did you see it? I only caught one glimpse, but I'll remember it forever. I saw the wind! The tops of the palm trees were spinning like giant wild birds, and their long leaves whipped around like angry tongues. I saw oranges flying through the air like a crazy game of catch. It's like the hurricane still remembers how to play even while it's raging! I saw men screaming at the masts of a ship. Their tiny lives! Why aren't they proud to die such an amazing death?

MISTRESS FAWCETT: Thank God Hamilton isn't among them!

RACHAEL: I'm telling you—if he were, the greatest man of his time would someday call you grandmother!

MISTRESS FAWCETT (forcing herself up): Listen to me, Rachael! Calm down! You've had your wild moment. I understand—you're throwing your feelings into the storm because you can't give them to Hamilton. But enough! I can't handle any more. I'm old. My heart is too weak. If I panic now, the storm will kill me.

RACHAEL: Very well, mother. I'll try to put my feelings away—if I can. Now's a good time; there's a break in the storm.

MISTRESS FAWCETT (sitting back down): Come here, Rachael. (Rachael, seeming calmer, walks over and stands beside her mother.

Gently, she fixes the old woman's hair, which had fallen loose during their struggle with the shutters.)

Rachael, these might be our last hours on earth. This house is old. The hurricane might tear it apart. Like you, I'm not afraid to die. In fact, I would welcome death tonight—if only you could go with me. What has hurt the most is the thought of leaving you alone.

I'm glad you finally broke your silence. I never could have broken it first. I want to ask you to forgive me. I admit that I alone caused the tragedy of your marriage. It's no excuse that I was fooled. I'm supposed to be smarter than most. I should have seen that behind that smooth, charming face was a cruel man. But I had always trusted the Danes, and you were the child of my old age. I knew I wouldn't live much longer.

Still, I'm not making excuses. I'm asking you, truly, to forgive me.

RACHAEL: Forgive you? I've always loved you with all my heart, and my mind has been trained in philosophy.

MISTRESS FAWCETT: Ah! I didn't know. You've always been so silent. And silent people—they think too much.

RACHAEL: I have thought, but I never blamed you. What's past is past. I don't waste time regretting what can't be undone. The soul has to be shaped and hardened—sometimes through pain, through being torn apart and beaten down. Let's hope that, having suffered early, I won't have to suffer like that again.

MISTRESS FAWCETT: There are worse things than a bad marriage. One is falling in love with a man you can never marry—and being thrown aside while you still love him, while your heart is still alive. Then you are alone, maybe with children, while the world looks at you with pity or judgment. Divorce brings a shame that's worse than death for some women.

Rachael—won't you promise me—?

RACHAEL: I promise that when I'm thinking clearly, I'll put you first. But if I ever meet Hamilton when I feel like I do tonight—then I wouldn't think at all. I wouldn't think or care! I'm not like those frightened people hiding in the cellar. Nature made me to love, to hate, to create, to suffer—to feel as wildly as the storm feels tonight!

MISTRESS FAWCETT (with a long, tired sigh): Thank heaven Hamilton isn't here. Ah!

RACHAEL: Yes, the storm is rising again.

[The hurricane crashes down with even greater force. It sounds like cannon fire. Hail slams against the roof. Trees and rooftops smash together in midair. Suddenly, the house shakes violently. At the same time, there's a long, terrible scream from the slaves hiding in the cellar.]

RACHAEL: Has the whole island been ripped from its roots?

MISTRESS FAWCETT: That was an earthquake. A hurricane pulls so hard it even stirs the ground. I just hope the fires in Nevis are out. But we can't worry about what might happen. Focus on the windows! (As Rachael checks the windows, Mistress Fawcett leans toward the front door, straining to listen. She slowly rises from her chair, her eyes wide, but keeps her face turned away from Rachael.)

I think I hear a shutter banging in the dining-room. Run and check. And check all the windows before you come back. If the wind gets inside, the roof will tear off. (Rachael runs out of the room.)

[Right after she leaves, there's a loud knock at the front door, which is on the side of the house protected from the worst of the storm.

Mistress Fawcett hobbles over and tightens the iron bar across the door, making sure no one can force their way in.]

MISTRESS FAWCETT: Who's there?

A VOICE OUTSIDE: It's me—James Hamilton.

MISTRESS FAWCETT: You cannot come in.

HAMILTON: Not come in? I risked my life to get here, knowing you were alone. You wouldn't even leave a dog outside on a day like this.

MISTRESS FAWCETT: I would open the door for the worst criminal in the islands, but not for you. Go! Go now! (She turns anxiously toward the row of rooms where Rachael is still checking the windows.) Surely she can't hear us—the wind is too loud. (Raising her voice again.) You cannot enter. If my daughter opens the door, it will only be after she has fought me for it. Will you leave—or at least stay silent? You can shelter under the veranda until the storm shifts, then find safety in an outhouse.

HAMILTON: There's no outhouse left standing. Not a stone on stone. Only this house is still here. Most of the trees are down too. If you send me away, you're sending me to certain death.

MISTRESS FAWCETT (in deep distress): What am I to do? I don't wish you dead. If I let you in, will you let me hide you? Will you promise not to show yourself to Rachael?

HAMILTON: I will not promise.

[Rachael enters. She lifts her head, sensing something.]

RACHAEL: Who is out there?

MISTRESS FAWCETT (turning sharply, standing tall, blocking the door): James Hamilton.

RACHAEL: Ah! (She moves quickly, but stops when she sees the meaning in her mother's face and stance.) Let him in!

MISTRESS FAWCETT: No.

RACHAEL: You can't mean it! He must be half dead by now. But no—you're just waiting to make me promise something first.

MISTRESS FAWCETT: Will you promise?

RACHAEL: No.

MISTRESS FAWCETT: Then he'll die out there in the storm. (Rachael laughs bitterly and steps toward the door. Mistress Fawcett raises her hand warningly.) If you try to fight me, it will kill me. You have to choose—him or me. (Rachael cries out and covers her face. Hamilton throws himself against the door, but the iron bar holds.)

HAMILTON: The wind is shifting, Mistress Fawcett. Can't you hear the stillness? In a moment, the hurricane will come back even stronger from the west. If you don't let me in, I'll stay right here and face it. I had to crawl here on my hands and knees—it took me two hours to move half a mile. I won't crawl back. I came to protect Rachael—or to die with her, if that's what happens.

MISTRESS FAWCETT: Or to destroy her life.

HAMILTON: That's already done.

MISTRESS FAWCETT: True. But I can protect her from more pain.

RACHAEL: Fine! Keep him out if you want. But you can't keep me in. I won't fight you, and I won't force my way through your door. But if you don't open it right now, I'll leave through another.

MISTRESS FAWCETT: Rachael! Don't I mean anything to you? I've loved you so much! Is this how you repay me?

RACHAEL: I know you love me. I don't take that lightly. But if women loved their mothers more than the men they loved, there would be no future generations. And what does it matter what we want compared to what Fate has already decided? Can't you see it? Why else would he have reached me tonight? What man has ever survived a hurricane before? Nature itself paused to let him through.

Do you really think you can fight that? Quick—answer me! (She half-turns toward the next room, ready to leave.)

MISTRESS FAWCETT: You've won. But wait until I'm out of the room. (She leans heavily on her crutch and slowly leaves. Rachael holds her breath until the door shuts behind her, then quickly rushes to the door and lifts the bar. Hamilton steps inside. His hat is gone, his long cape torn and covered in leaves and dirt. He quickly shuts and bars the door again. Seeing him safely inside, Rachael's feelings shift. She steps back, grabs a pan of coals from the corner, lights them, and quickly starts mixing a hot drink.)

RACHAEL (hurriedly): You're freezing. You must be exhausted. I'll get you something warm right away.

[Hamilton looks at her for a long moment, then drops heavily into a chair by the table, rubbing his head.]

HAMILTON: Thank you. I feel like the whole hurricane is spinning inside my head.

RACHAEL (pouring the drink into a silver goblet): Here. Drink this.

HAMILTON: Gladly. (He raises the goblet.) Here's to the hurricane.

[Rachael keeps moving nervously around the room, staying across the table from him.]

RACHAEL: Tell me about your journey here. I'm surprised you don't look like an old man. Ah, your color's coming back—you already look young again.

HAMILTON (after draining the goblet, setting it down, and standing to face her): Did you ever doubt I would come?

RACHAEL (speaking lightly, avoiding his eyes): I thought you were still on St. Kitts.

HAMILTON (intensely): Even then, I would have come. I knew this storm would bring me to you. Out there, battling the wind, almost ripped apart, I still knew it. Nature was forcing me toward you, just like it kept us apart with all that awful calm before.

RACHAEL (half-laughing, half-despairing): And even after that nightmare, you still have the strength for love and poetry? I'd just want a bed to collapse into. Tomorrow—tomorrow—we'll sit out on the terrace and pretend none of this ever happened.

HAMILTON: Rachael! I didn't fight my way here to joke around.

RACHAEL: I need to go to my mother! She's alone! What have I done?

HAMILTON: Stay! Do you regret opening the door?

[Rachael hesitates, then lifts her eyes and answers clearly.]

RACHAEL: No.

[She leans on the table, still keeping it between them. Hamilton leans forward and clasps her wrists tightly.]

HAMILTON: This hurricane is either an ending—or a new beginning.

RACHAEL (lifting her head proudly): A beginning!

HAMILTON: Yes. This storm has come to help us, not to destroy us—no matter what happens now. (His voice is rough and slow. They stare at each other without speaking, breathless. Hamilton's pressure slowly pushes the table aside.)

RACHAEL: Listen!

HAMILTON: Yes—the storm is back.

[Suddenly, the hurricane slams into the house harder than ever. The whole building shakes. From below, the slaves scream in terror. Water crashes against the roof. The roar grows louder and louder until it feels like the very noise could tear the world apart. Hamilton pushes the table out of the way and pulls Rachael tightly into his arms. Her joyful, triumphant laugh rises up and mixes with the furious howl of the storm.]

Talbot of Ursula

(This story first appeared in the Anglo-Saxon Review, and is republished by kind permission of Mrs. George Cornwallis-West)

I

The Señora, as usual, had sent a short, formal note that morning, inviting John Talbot to have his birthday dinner at the Rancho de los Olivos. Even though he visited her once a week all year long, she normally offered him nothing more than a glass of angelica wine or a cup of chocolate. But for his birthday, she made a real feast. A turkey was killed, and her old cook prepared so many hot dishes and sweet desserts from the old days that Talbot ended up feeling sick for three days. Still, he would have gladly suffered for six if it meant he could enjoy the meal—and the brief feeling of family life that came with it.

In Santa Ursula, the Señora and the Mission padre were Talbot's only real friends, though for political reasons he sometimes visited the village saloon and chatted with the mixed crowd there about whatever news managed to reach their remote corner of California. Yet Talbot had lived in Santa Ursula for twenty-three years without leaving, except for short trips to San Francisco, Sacramento, and a few towns in the South.

Why had he stayed in such a lonely, forgotten place even after becoming rich? As he paced the corridor of the Mission on his fortieth birthday, he asked himself that question again—he had asked it many times before.

For some, the peacefulness and warm, sleepy beauty of the area would have been answer enough. Two brown-robed friars walked past him, reading prayers. Beyond the arches of the corridor, the land dropped sharply away from the Mission, revealing a vast valley stretching all the way to the horizon, broken only by the Santa Barbara mountains to the east. The sun burned fiercely in a deep blue sky, and under its heat the endless olive orchard below shimmered like a silver sea. The bright waves of the trees met the sky sharply and curled against the foothills. Watching a bird glide low and then rise again, Talbot almost expected to see it shake off drops of silver. He sighed, thinking how cool it must be in the shady groves below—much cooler than he would be during his long ride under the brutal midday sun. Then he remembered the Señora's cool, dark living room, and that part of the trip would take him through shady cottonwoods and willows along the river. He smiled to himself. He had learned long ago to survive Santa Ursula with a good sense of humor.

There was one dark, forested mountain near the Mission, with only a rough trail leading to the top. Few people had ever climbed it, but Talbot knew it well. Hidden at the summit was a small lake, so clear it reflected every pine needle surrounding it.

West of the Mission, past the river and beyond a dusty road winding through fields, hills, and canyons, stood the old adobe house of the Rancho de los Olivos.

Talbot was a very practical man these days. He owned the vast olive orchard, the small hotel at the end of the plateau, and all the land where the rough village had grown up—with its store, saloon, post office, and scattered shacks. He was also involved in bigger politics, having served two years in the State Legislature and now being talked about as a future Senator.

It couldn't be said that the people of Santa Ursula loved him—he was too reserved, never the type to slap a man on the back. It was rumored that he subscribed to a San Francisco newspaper but selfishly kept it to himself, and that he owned a big collection of books locked away in one of his Mission rooms. As far as anyone could tell, the priest was his only true companion.

Still, even though some people didn't like how distant he was, they respected him. For twenty-three years, he had never broken a promise or taken advantage of anyone. Even those who disliked how cold he seemed admitted that if he ever held higher office, California's interests would be safe with him. Some even thought it would be smart to keep him in Congress for life, the way some New England states did with their best leaders. At the very least, they planned to send him to the House of Representatives for a few terms and, if he proved himself, eventually to the U.S. Senate.

Santa Ursula only had one street, but its saloon was the lively center for a hundred miles around. It was proud of Talbot—proud enough to puff up like an old Spanish don. When the Legislature nicknamed him "Talbot of Ursula," to tell him apart from two other Talbots, the little town's pride in him reached new heights. The title stuck, and he carried it for the rest of his life.

It wasn't until a newspaper interviewed John Talbot after he was elected to the State Senate that people found out he had been born in England. But since he had moved to America with his parents when he was fourteen, and because the district was filled with Germans, Irish, Swedes, Mexicans, and Italians, no one really cared. Besides, Talbot had built his own fortune—with just a little help from an uncle—and he was fully American in every way. England, to him, was nothing more than a faraway, peaceful dream, like a place you only visit after life is over. He remembered almost nothing from those early years—except for one moment that had shaped his entire life.

That memory stayed with him, even though it seemed out of place on this hot, still morning by the Southern sea. He was standing near the old white Mission with its red-tiled roof and silver bells, which once called hundreds of Native Americans to prayer. The bells still rang loudly, but few people answered them now. Still, the memory rose up and held him tight.

Back in England, his mother, a widow, had run a small shop in their village. John had gone to school from a very young age. Because he had grown fast and was often sickly, he had spent more time in his books than roughhousing with the other boys. But he loved learning, and the other boys were kind to him, so he had been pretty happy with his life.

One day, though, his mother told him to put on his best clothes and come with her to a wedding. John protested—he was in the middle of a good book—but he obeyed, pulling on his Sunday outfit and following his mother and the other women up to the old stone church on top of the hill. The daughter of the local noble family was getting married that day, and all the little girls John knew were dressed in white, tossing flower petals along the main street and up to the castle gates. John thought it was all a silly waste of good flowers, but he stood in the crowd, feeling a little curious.

When the bride arrived in an open carriage and walked down the path to the church, John stared at her with wide eyes and an open mouth. It wasn't just that she was beautiful—he had seen pretty women before—but she carried herself with a kind of proud grace he had never seen. She moved so lightly and seemed so far above his own world that it took his breath away. She didn't seem real.

When she disappeared into the church, he glanced around at the village girls and even his mother, and they all suddenly looked plain and rough. When the bride came out again, he noticed there were other girls in her group who had the same light, graceful look. That stunned him even more. She wasn't one of a kind after all—there was a whole world of people like her. Filled with excitement, he broke away from his mother and ran after the carriage for nearly a mile, trying to hold onto the sight of her. The bride noticed him, smiled, and threw him a rose. He still had that rose.

A week later, he told his mother he planned to marry a lady when he grew up. She stared at him, then laughed. But when he repeated it a few nights later, she told him firmly to forget about it—boys like him didn't marry ladies. She explained it very bluntly, and John felt crushed.

But soon after, when his mother announced they were moving to America, she said, almost casually, "Maybe you'll get your wish out there. I've heard that in America, one person is as good as another. If you're a good boy and make lots of money, you can marry a lady just like anyone else." She forgot she said it—but John never did.

Not long after they arrived in New York, his mother died. His uncle sent him to school for two years, and then one day told him to pack his things. They were heading to California to search for gold. They bought a sturdy wagon and joined a large group crossing the plains in search of fortune.

That trip across the wild country was the adventure of John's life. They fought off Native American attacks three times, and two people in their group were killed. John always felt young again when he remembered those days. It had been one of those rare moments when life felt exactly the way it should—dangerous, exciting, and full of hope.

John and his uncle stayed in the San Joaquin Valley for about a year. They didn't strike it rich like some others, but they still left with a few thousand dollars. They moved to San Francisco, where Mr. Quick opened a gambling house and saloon. He made money much faster there than he had in the valley—mostly because he had lost a lot at night what he had earned during the day. Even though he wasn't the most honest man, he was a responsible uncle, and soon sent John out to the countryside to manage a ranch near the Mission of Santa Ursula.

John never knew that the land had been won in a card game from Don Roberto Ortega, one of the wildest rich landowners in California. The land grant covered about fifty thousand acres, and it had a few small olive orchards already planted. John, using his own money, planted twelve thousand more acres with olive trees on the part that his uncle had won. They were supposed to be partners, and John would eventually inherit his uncle's share too. But when Mr. Quick married a Mexican woman who later stabbed him and ran off with what little money he had saved, John was left with nothing but the land.

John worked hard. Every time he saved a little money, he bought more land in San Francisco. He ended up supplying almost the entire state of California with olives and olive oil, and over time, he became a wealthy man.

And his dream of marrying a "lady"? It didn't die—not from fighting Native Americans, not from the wild life of San Francisco, not from hard work among his olive trees, or even from his growing fortune and importance. The dream stayed alive until a real woman— with a voice as silver as the olive leaves—laughed it out of him. She left him strong, handsome, and still unmarried at forty.

At first, when John moved to the Mission, there were no women around. The nearby ranch house was empty, and there wasn't even a village yet. John spent his time working with his olive trees and spending evenings with the priests, who had taken him in like family. He also spent hours studying law and his favorite subject, political economy. Even though he was good-looking, with a sun-browned, finely shaped face and strong figure, the priests never guessed that he was a romantic at heart.

John rarely spoke of women. He only once told the priests how glad he was to be away from the wild women of San Francisco. None of them could have imagined that while he worked, John often dreamed about the day a real lady would come into his life and make him the happiest man on earth.

John was twenty when he finally met Delfina Carillo. Don Roberto Ortega had died before he could lose the rest of his fortune, and his widow, who was weak and ill, left their ranch near Monterey to move south into the hotter climate. She brought her son, Don Enrique, with her. John saw Don Enrique riding around the countryside morning and night, sometimes stopping by the Mission for a drink. Don Enrique was a striking figure: slim, dark, with large soft eyes, fancy silk clothes, a flashy silver-trimmed sombrero, and a saddle so loaded with silver that only a strong horse could carry it.

John wasn't impressed. He thought Don Enrique looked like a stage actor or a circus rider. Still, he was curious about the life of the wealthy Californians, about whom he had heard so much but seen so little. When Padre Ortega, who was related to the Ortegas, invited John to a ball that would kick off a season of parties at the ranch, John began to look forward to it with the excitement only youth can feel.

But John didn't just sit around dreaming. He went to San Francisco and bought a proper wardrobe for the occasion. It was American-style, not Californian—John wouldn't have worn silk and lace even if he were the richest man alive.

Since the stagecoach didn't go all the way to Santa Ursula, a servant met him twenty miles from home with a horse and a cart for his trunk. John washed off the dust of three days' travel in a creek, mounted his big gray mare, and started for home at a happy gallop.

The morning was brilliant, the world was fresh and full of promise, and he felt like singing. He was riding one of the best horses in California, and life was opening up before him like a dream. He wasn't afraid of the upcoming social event. By now, he had the American sense of confidence. He hadn't heard anyone use the word "gentleman" in years, his education was solid, he owned land, and he fully intended to become rich and successful. No wonder he felt like shouting for joy.

He had been riding for about eight or ten miles without seeing another soul in the wide, empty land of early California when he suddenly pulled his horse to a stop and listened. He was riding down into a narrow canyon. On the far side, the road kept going toward the interior; his path would soon turn sharply south when he crossed the narrow stream at the bottom.

Across the hills, he heard many voices—young, lighthearted, and laughing. John remembered that Doña Martina's guests were supposed to arrive that day, and he quickly guessed he was about to meet one of the groups. Young Californians loved traveling on horseback back then, and thought nothing of riding forty miles even under the burning summer sun. John, who was usually very modest, felt grateful that he was wearing a clean new suit of gray serge and had washed off the dust of travel earlier at the creek.

The group appeared at the top of the hill, riding down into the canyon. John raised his cap politely, and the young men responded with a dramatic sweep of their silver-trimmed sombreros. It would be a few minutes before they met, so John took the chance to enjoy the colorful scene. Suddenly, life felt strange and dreamlike to him. He forgot all about his olive trees and remembered the old stories the priests had told him about the wealthy Californian dons before America took over the land.

The young men were dressed head-to-toe in bright silk, looking more colorful than a summer garden. Their white shirts and silver decorations sparkled in the sun, and their horses—with their golden coats and silver manes and tails—looked like they had stepped out of a fairy tale, made just to match their riders.

The girls weren't as flashy. They wore delicate, flowered dresses and silk scarves wrapped around their heads instead of the silver-decorated sombreros. But they were the ones who caught John's attention. They had long black braids, glowing white skin, and dark sparkling eyes. From where he was, they all looked beautiful. But it wasn't just their beauty that made John's heart race and his face flush. This was one of the first times since that childhood wedding in his old village that he had seen real gentlewomen—and he knew this was his chance.

Excited and nervous, he spurred his horse down the hill, then paused again to watch them make their way through the golden grass and green bushes of the canyon.

Soon he spotted Don Enrique Ortega, who greeted him warmly as he rode into the creek and let his horse drink. John and Enrique had met at the Mission before. Even though Enrique saw Americans as an inferior people, he thought John was decent enough—and it was smart not to make enemies.

"Ah, Don Juan," Enrique said brightly, "you've been to Yerba Buena—what you call San Francisco now, eh? I'm meeting my friends who honor the Rancho de los Olivos with their visit. May I introduce you? You are a friend of my cousin, Padre Ortega."

The group had spread out along the creek to water their horses, creating a ribbon of color through the shadowed canyon. Enrique led John from person to person, introducing him solemnly to everyone. The young men loudly promised eternal friendship, though John knew they didn't mean a word of it. The girls smiled at him, flashing their bright teeth and dark eyes, but kept the proud, distant attitude that came from their high Spanish blood. No matter how good-looking John was, to them he was still an outsider—an American.

The girls all looked somewhat alike, their heads wrapped tightly in silk scarves. John instantly fell in love with all of them. He could pick one later. For now, he was too thrilled to think seriously about marriage. But in his heart, he decided he would win one of them.

He rode out of the canyon with the group, and they were friendly, chattering about the upcoming parties at the Rancho de los Olivos.

John noticed that Enrique kept close to one girl, riding a little ahead with her. She was tall and slender, and she moved so gracefully that when branches hung low, she would bend almost to her horse's neck. John was dying to see her face.

"That is Delfina Carillo," said the girl riding beside him, following his gaze. "I think she will marry Enrique. He's very devoted, and I think she likes him, but she hasn't said so."

Maybe it was just that she seemed a little more distant than the others, but John couldn't take his eyes off her. His curiosity burned, and he urged his companion to tell him more about her. He learned that Delfina was the daughter of a rich rancher near Santa Barbara and was the most admired young woman in the whole region.

"She has taken the place of Chonita Iturbi y Moncada," the girl explained. "Many caballeros want to marry her, but she pays little attention—except maybe to Enrique. Oh, he sings so beautifully, señor! No wonder she loves him. He serenades her every night with his music."

John thought to himself with amusement, "It must be the music—because he certainly doesn't have much else to offer."

He didn't actually see her until that night. The priest wore his brown robe to the ball, and John wore his formal black coat. Both of them looked out of place among the brightly dressed guests.

Doña Martina, large, dark-skinned, with a mustache and lots of jewelry, sat against the wall with other older women. They wore heavy red and yellow satin dresses, while the younger girls floated by in lighter silk gowns that fluttered when they moved.

Doña Martina greeted John sleepily, and he turned his attention to the dancing, though he didn't join in. He knew his manners were good and he carried himself well, but dancing had never been one of his skills.

Just then, a girl was dancing alone in the middle of the room, and John somehow knew right away it was Delfina Carillo. Like the other girls, she wore her hair up under a tall comb, but her dress was white and trimmed with fine Spanish lace. Her tiny feet showed a little as she danced, but it looked effortless—more like she was swaying in a light breeze, like moss in the trees.

The room had been quiet when she started dancing, but soon the young men began to mutter, then clap and stamp their feet. Finally, they threw gold and silver coins at her feet, shouting their excitement.

Delfina didn't seem to notice, except for a small flare of her nostrils; she kept dancing like something made of air and light.

Her beauty was almost shocking. Even though John was still young, he knew he might never see such perfect beauty again. Her face wasn't especially thoughtful, but every line was flawless, her coloring soft and delicate. Her huge black eyes were framed with lashes so long they almost tangled. Her skin was pale, her lips and cheeks pink, and her mouth curved gently. Her figure, arms, hands, and feet were all shaped so perfectly they seemed to express more than her face ever could. John also noticed she had a proud tilt to her nose, a short upper lip, and a way of carrying herself that showed both hidden and open pride.

She glided off the dance floor without glancing at the coins on the ground, and John knew in that moment he loved her completely. She was everything his romantic heart had ever dreamed of. For a second, he felt almost faint thinking of the obstacles between them—but he was young and hopeful. He shook off his fear and asked right away to be introduced.

When they met, Delfina's dark eyes slid over his face with little interest, but something in his intense gaze caught her attention. She didn't seem eager to talk, but she smiled once or twice—and when she smiled, she was dazzling.

"That dance was incredible, señorita. But doesn't it make you tired?" John asked.

"No," she answered simply.

"I suppose you're happy to bring so much pleasure to others?"

"Si," she said again, barely glancing at him.

"You must hear a lot of compliments," John said, "but I have to tell you—that was the most beautiful thing I've ever seen. And I've traveled quite a bit."

"Si?" she answered politely but without much interest.

"I wish I could dance," he said. "Even if it was just once—with you."

"You don't dance?" she asked, her voice sounding a little amused, even though it was barely above a whisper.

"Would you—" John hesitated, "would you at least talk with me during a dance?"

"Oh no," she said, clearly shocked. It was as if he had asked her to lock herself away for the whole night. She turned gracefully away, lifted her hand to Enrique's shoulder, and a moment later was dancing down the room with him. John noticed that her cheeks were slightly pinker than before.

"It's impossible," he thought, "that she truly cares for that fool."

But as the days passed, John realized he was going to have a tough fight ahead. He was invited to all the parties and gatherings. They had picnics among the cottonwoods and hills, danced every night, were entertained by the priests, and enjoyed bullfights, horse races, and contests of skill. John even hosted a moonlight dance in his own olive groves.

Enrique made no secret of his devotion to Delfina, and every night he sang love songs under her window. Sometimes John, riding restlessly around the ranch unable to sleep, would hear Enrique's sweet voice serenading her—and he would curse so loudly he scared the night birds.

Still, John found ways to stay close to Delfina too, even when Enrique shot him dirty looks. Enrique didn't worry much about Americans, thinking them too far beneath him to be a real threat.

John managed to have several private talks with Delfina, and he soon realized something disappointing: she wasn't very deep. She hadn't read much, barely thought about anything serious. Her mind was mostly focused on her place in society. Still, she was kind in her own proud way and surprisingly unselfish for someone so privileged.

John didn't care. He was deep in his first real passion, and he loved with everything he had. Even if she had been silly or shallow, he wouldn't have cared. She was beautiful, magnetic, and the perfect image of all he had ever dreamed of. And as his love grew stronger, it had nothing to do with ambition or pride. He simply wanted her—and even if he learned she wasn't a true noblewoman, but just an ordinary girl, it wouldn't have changed his feelings one bit.

His olive trees were left to grow wild, and he spent all his free time riding across the countryside, pushing his horses as hard as any Californian. Sometimes, moved by the love she saw in his eyes, Delfina would soften for a moment and ask him a question or two — a rare gift from someone who usually said so little. Once, when John lifted her down from her horse under the thick shade of the trees, she gave him such a powerful look that he rushed away, afraid he might make a fool of himself in front of everyone. Still, he wasn't truly unhappy. Even though the feelings of love, hope, and fear tore through him, they felt sweet because they were so new and exciting.

Then, one night, everything changed.

Delfina said she wanted to see the hidden lake at the top of the lonely mountain. The Indians had found it long ago, but the rich Californians had never bothered to climb up there. The group was sitting on the long porch of the Ortega house when Delfina surprised Enrique by ordering him to lead them there that very night.

"But, my lady," Enrique said nervously, "there's no real path. I don't even know the way! It's as steep as the Mission tower!"

John stepped forward. "There's an old Indian trail," he said. "I've climbed it before. But it's narrow and steep."

Delfina's eyes, which had been full of anger at Enrique, softened when she looked at John. "We will go with you," she said, "tonight, since the moon is full. And I will ride by your side."

John glanced up at the tall mountain, still wild and untouched, and thought this could be the happiest night of his life. They quickly rode ahead of the others, so close their shoulders brushed. The full moon lit up the sky, but the forest around them was mostly dark, with only patches of silver light. It felt like they were alone in a wild, forgotten world — except for the distant laughter behind them. Delfina had never been more charming. She even spoke a little, though her way of flirting didn't need many words. A tilt of her head or a change in her voice said more than a whole conversation. John felt dizzy with emotion but held back, waiting for the right moment.

When they reached the lake, it looked like a second moon resting at the top of the mountain, with the dark trees circling just around the edges. The view was so breathtaking that everyone fell silent, the mountaintop as still as it had been for hundreds of years. Then someone shouted, "Ay, yi!" and soon others joined in: "Dios de mi alma!" "Dios de mi vida!" "Ay, California! California!" "Ay, de mi, de mi, de mi!"

While the others were busy admiring the view, John grabbed Delfina's horse and led her into the shadows of the forest. His words spilled out in a rush.

"I have to tell you—I must!" he said, barely able to keep his voice steady. "I know I haven't had time to make you love me, but I love you! I love you! I want to marry you! Oh—I can't even breathe!" He yanked at his collar, feeling like the whole mountain was spinning around him.

Delfina threw her head back. "Ay!" she said, and then she laughed.

She didn't mean to hurt him, but her laugh cut right through John's heart. He shook all over. His pale face stood out clearly in the dim light, and Delfina stopped laughing and spoke softly.

"Poor boy," she said kindly. "I'm sorry if I hurt you. But I can't marry you. I could never love an American. You're not like our men — so handsome, so graceful, so grand. I like you — you're a nice boy — but I'm going to marry Enrique. So don't think about it anymore."

As John stood there, crushed and silent, she leaned forward and added gently, "You can kiss me once if you want. You are just a boy to me, so I don't mind."

John kissed her with all the wild, hopeless love in his heart — a kiss so full of pain and longing that Delfina never forgot it.

After that, John never went back to the Ortega house. He hid among his olive trees whenever the party from Los Olivos rode by the Mission. A week later, Delfina returned home, and three months later she came back as Enrique Ortega's wife.

John smiled a little as he thought about the boy he had once been. There had been months when he had felt almost crazy with heartbreak. Then came years of sadness and a growing hatred for everything except hard work. He couldn't bring himself to sell the ranch and leave. Somehow, he clung to the place where everything had fallen apart.

He didn't see Delfina again for three years. By then, she had three children and had started to grow heavy. Yet she was still very beautiful, and John stayed away for a few more years.

But time moved on. Doña Martina died. So did six of Delfina's ten children. Then Enrique died too, leaving behind his shrinking estate, his widow, and their four little daughters — all under the care of John Talbot.

This happened after fourteen years of marriage and six years of friendship between John and the family at Los Olivos. One day, desperate because of land troubles with squatters, Enrique had turned to John for help. John found him a good lawyer, loaned him money, and helped him win back his land. Enrique was so grateful that he insisted John be treated like part of the family. Over time, the two men became true friends.

Enrique and Delfina lived a quiet, steady life together. Delfina had been a loyal wife, a loving mother, and a proud but practical housekeeper. Enrique had been a kind, easygoing husband. Even though they didn't talk much, when they did, their conversations were friendly. Enrique never grew into a clever man, but he was always a good host and took polite interest in the world around him. John soon got used to visiting Los Olivos twice a week, always bringing candies for the little girls, who loved him more than they did their own father.

And what about John's old love for Delfina? He often told himself it was buried deep inside her now, hidden under the passing years and the weight she had gained. She now weighed about two hundred pounds. Her black hair and beautiful teeth were all that remained of the stunning girl he had once loved. Her face had grown large and brown, but she still carried herself with the same slow, graceful pride. Now, she looked exactly like what she was — the proud Spanish mother of many children.

The change in John's heart had come slowly, without much pain. He had a strong memory, and sometimes when he thought back to his younger days and his one great love, he felt a small ache — just a faint reminder of the old heartbreak. But it was only a shadow of what it had once been. He had moved on a long time ago. Sometimes he wondered why he never fell in love again, or why his dream of marrying a noblewoman had died with that first love. He decided it was because all the deep emotions he once had were used up during those hard years, leaving him unable to feel that way again. Now he knew that marrying without real love would be hollow and pointless.

Now and then, after visiting the Señora — that wide, coffee-colored woman waving to him from her doorway — he would sigh and remember the beautiful young girl he had once loved. But even those sighs had become rare. Time had buried that dream deep, and he was now too busy and practical to dwell on the past. Besides, Señora Ortega had become his closest friend. What she lacked in cleverness, she made up for with kindness and loyalty, and over the years, she had grown a bit wiser too. It had become easy for him to talk to her about his plans and ambitions, especially after Enrique's death, when they spent many long, quiet hours together.

When Enrique died, Talbot quickly stepped in to manage the estate. The Señora trusted him completely and never even asked about the details of her finances. One by one, the daughters got married, and John provided dowries for each of them. They were lovely young women, and he loved them all because each one carried a trace of the beauty he had once seen in Delfina. Sometimes they reminded him of his old heartbreak, but they also reminded him of the sweet memories. The Señora herself, though, stirred no such feelings anymore.

For the past year, she had been living alone. Two of her daughters had moved to Mexico City. Another had married a Spanish consul and moved to Spain. One more lived in San Francisco and planned to visit her sisters when she could. When Talbot was at home, he made it a point to visit the Señora once a week, always bringing her a new novel or an illustrated magazine tucked into his saddlebag.

"Where does the real sadness lie?" Talbot wondered as he walked back and forth along the Mission's cool hallway on his fortieth birthday. "That I couldn't have her when I loved her with all my heart, or that I could have her now and feel nothing?"

He knew the Señora was lonely in her big, empty house and would have gladly welcomed a companion. But he also knew her wish was slow and passive — if he showed interest, she would accept it; if not, it wouldn't trouble her much.

Just then, his Indian servant rode up with his horse. Talbot took one last look at the shaded Mission corridor, then rode out into the blazing sunlight.

He wasn't much heavier than he had been years ago, but he rode more carefully now. His favorite mare was older too, and he no longer had the energy for breaking wild mustangs. He preferred a calm, dependable horse that matched his quieter life.

The road by the river, shaded by cottonwoods and willows, was almost cool and comfortable. But once he left the river, he faced five long miles of sun-scorched fields and hills that gleamed like polished gold. The dark blue sky looked like metal, with the sun burning fiercely through a hole in it. The heat shimmered above the ground, and the mountains floated in a purple haze. Talbot tucked a grape leaf into his hat for a little extra shade, but even after years under the California sun, he still wished — as he often did — that his birthday came in winter instead of summer.

After riding for about an hour and a half, he finally reached the shady grounds of Casa Ortega. He nudged his horse to move faster, grateful for the cooler air under the huge oak trees. A Mexican servant came to meet him, and Talbot got down and walked the rest of the way to the house. He sighed as he remembered how Herminia, the last daughter to marry, had been there to greet him with a birthday kiss just one year ago. He would have gladly welcomed all four girls back again, but now they were gone from his life for good.

The Casa Ortega was a long, low adobe house, only one story tall and just one room deep, except for a section in the back where several rooms were grouped together. Every year, the Señora made sure it was whitewashed and the red tiles on the roof were repaired when needed. Because of her care, the house still looked fresh and strong, unlike many other old adobe homes that had fallen into sad decay after the grand old families faded away.

A long porch stretched across the front of the house, supported by pillars and decorated with brightly painted chairs. But the porch was empty, and Talbot went straight into the sala. It was a long room, simply furnished in the old Spanish style. Across from the door hung a portrait of Delfina Carillo. Talbot rarely let himself look at it. If he had been brave enough, he would have asked the Señora to take it down. Time had buried his love, but some ghosts still lingered.

The Señora was sitting quietly in a corner of the cool, dim room. She stood up right away to greet him, moving with a graceful dignity that still stirred his admiration. But she had grown very dark, and the beautiful smile he remembered had long since disappeared into the heavy cheeks and broad chin. Even her famous big eyes looked smaller now, and the once-thick lashes had thinned after many years of weeping — six of her children lay buried in the churchyard, and she had loved them dearly. She carried her two hundred pounds with the same ease she had once carried her slim, willowy figure. She always wore soft black cashmere in winter and light lawn dresses in summer, fastened at the neck with a tiny portrait of her late husband. Though she was only thirty-nine, there was not a trace of youth left in her. Her whole presence gave off the feeling of a life fully lived, and a quiet acceptance of it.

Talbot sometimes wondered if she ever felt crushing loneliness, but she never showed it. He figured that books and religion were enough to fill her days.

"So hot today, no?" she said softly, her voice still gentle and sweet, just like her manner. "Your face is very red. But you feel better soon. It is very cool here, no?"

"I already feel ten years younger than I did fifteen minutes ago," Talbot said, smiling. "There was a time — too long ago — when I could stand the California sun for six hours straight without minding it."

"Ay, yes, we grow more old every year. Twenty years now since we had the meriendas all day and danced all night — when I was only a visitor here, and you were the thin boy with the long arms and legs, trying to grow a mustache."

It was the first time she had ever spoken about their youth, and Talbot stared at her in surprise. But her face was as calm and peaceful as if she were simply offering him a plate of chicken with chile sauce.

He glanced, almost without thinking, at the portrait. It seemed full of life, and in the dim light, he imagined the eyes looked almost sad.

"How can she bear it?" he thought. "How can she stand it?"

"You have improved," the Señora said politely. "American men don't grow old the way Spanish men do—or women who have ten children and so many troubles."

"You still have kept much, Señora," Talbot said awkwardly, stumbling over what was probably the first compliment he had ever paid her.

She smiled gently and moved her head slowly — "shaking" didn't seem the right word for her graceful motions. "I have the mirror—and the picture. And I don't mind, Don Juan. When a woman buries six children, she no longer cares if she grows old. The sooner old age comes, the sooner she will die and see her little ones again. I loved Enrique very much too," she added, "but when we were young, I loved him even more. He was a good man, always, but he grew old like me and grew very fat. Only you have improved, my friend. That's one reason I am always so glad to see you. You remind me of the time when we were all young and happy."

Old Marcia came in then to announce dinner, and Talbot jumped to his feet, feeling a wave of relief. He offered the Señora his arm. She made no more comments about the past during their meal. Instead, they talked about the crops and the latest political news. She listened carefully, knowing politics had become Talbot's biggest passion, and even though she realized that someday his career might take him far away, she never tried to hold him back. Her days of living for herself were long over.

When they finished the last dulce, they went out to the veranda and chatted sleepily about small matters until both drifted into naps in their chairs.

At first, Talbot's full stomach weighed him down, but after a while, he began to dream. His dreams brought back memories of his youth — vivid images of Delfina, glowing with beauty and laughter. The morning's memories had seemed distant and faded, but now they burned in his mind with painful clarity. He relived the highs and lows of that passionate time, and the light of those old feelings seemed to flood through him again.

He woke up suddenly. The Señora was still sleeping nearby, her face as calm as ever. It had softened slightly with sleep, but she didn't yet have the loose features of old age. Still, she looked so large and brown and heavy that Talbot got up abruptly, feeling a stab of the old heartbreak. He walked into the sala and stood facing the portrait.

It was a fine painting. The background gave it a sense of depth, and in the dim light, it almost looked alive. The mouth curved in a faint smile, the eyes sparkled with youth and pride, and the skin was as pale as the moonflowers that grew in the fields at night.

Talbot remembered the night he had once held this young woman in his arms — not the woman sleeping on the porch now — and without thinking, he lifted his arms toward the painting.

"And I thought it was all over," he whispered shakily. "But I'd give everything I have — even my soul — if she could step out of that frame and love me again for just one hour."

"What are you saying?" came a soft, sleepy voice behind him. "I fell asleep, no? If you ring that little bell, Marcia will bring us some chocolate. Too hot outside for you?"

"No, no," he said quickly. "I like it better out here. It's cooler now, and I need all the air I can get."

He wanted badly to leave, but he stayed and sipped the chocolate Marcia brought, listening politely as the Señora talked about her daughters and grandchildren, whose photos were scattered everywhere around the house.

At six o'clock, Talbot shook her hand, mounted his horse, and rode away. As always, halfway down the avenue, he turned to look back. She was still standing on the porch, smiling warmly, her big brown hand waving slowly.

It was the last time he ever saw her.

II

Talbot had to leave for San Francisco a few days later, and when he returned, he found out that the Señora was sick in bed with a bad cold. He sent her a box of books and magazines, along with another box filled with chocolates. After that, though, he got caught up in the excitement of the elections and didn't think much about her for a while. It was the fall of 1868, and Talbot was a strong supporter of General Grant. He traveled all over the state, giving speeches to rally support for Grant, and with each success, Talbot's own reputation grew bigger. The more victories he helped achieve, the more he fell in love with politics. Eventually, he announced that he would run for Congress in the next election. But just two days later, when a congressman from his district passed away, Talbot was immediately appointed to take his place.

When he left for Washington at the end of November, the Señora was still in bed, fighting the same stubborn cold. He rode over to say goodbye to old Marcia, the housekeeper, and arranged for a San

Francisco bookstore to send the Señora a steady supply of illustrated papers and magazines.

During the busy months that followed in Washington, the Señora barely crossed his mind. Talbot finally realized that politics was his true calling, and he decided to stay in it for the rest of his life. The early months in Washington were filled with tension. Rumors swirled that Grant might be assassinated during his inauguration, but thankfully, nothing happened. Talbot was proud to have been there to witness that historic day. He even wrote the Señora a long letter about the military parades and the grand scene in the Senate, but she no longer held the same important place in his thoughts.

And since he was a wealthy, good-looking bachelor now firmly established in political life, he quickly found himself swept into Washington society. For the first time since his days at Los Olivos, he genuinely enjoyed being around people. San Francisco's social life had always felt like a cheap copy of what he had read about in books, but Washington was the real thing. It was full of brilliant conversation and elegant women.

He met more than one woman who reminded him of the dreamy ideal he had carried in his heart since boyhood — women who, in truth, resembled his old dream more closely than Delfina Carillo ever had. Delfina had been beautiful, but she had never been like the English girl he had seen in the village churchyard back home — the first image that had shaped his young hopes.

It was a long, busy session, and Talbot poured all his energy into the great issue of Reconstruction. Still, sometimes he asked himself if it wasn't time to think about marriage — to finally give his younger self what he had once wanted so badly. A beautiful, refined wife would surely still bring him happiness. Over the years in San Francisco, he had had more than one chance to marry charming young women, but the deep wound left by his first love had made him wary of marrying without strong feelings. Now, in Washington, far from California, still young and full of life at forty, he wondered if it was possible to fall in love again.

Surely life allowed a man more than one beginning. Often, when sitting in a lovely woman's parlor or standing close beside a charming girl under the soft lights of a conservatory, he found himself hoping for the old thrilling rush of hope and fear. He decided he would let himself fall in love at the first true sign of it. But it never came. He remained entertained and interested — but not shaken. The passionate waters inside him had calmed too much. No matter how he tried, he couldn't stir them up again.

Meanwhile, it wasn't surprising that the Señora didn't write. She hated writing letters and only forced herself to send one each month to her daughters, always with heavy sighs of protest. Padre Ortega was too old to keep up a correspondence either. So Talbot received little news from Santa Ursula, except for dry reports from his ranch manager, who updated him once a month about the olive trees and the hotel. The man wasn't one for gossip, and despite a few letters of inquiry, Talbot stayed in the dark about the Señora's health.

Finally, near the end of the congressional session, a note at the bottom of one report caught Talbot's eye:

The Señora is dying, I think — the quick kind of consumption. You might get to see her again, or maybe not. Everyone here feels bad about it. She was always good and fair to everyone.

There were still three weeks left in the session, but Talbot's committee work was finished, and he was free to leave. He made a deal with a friendly Democrat to cover his vote and left for California the same day he got the letter.

His decision to go to the Señora's bedside came instantly, without hesitation. He forgot all about the glittering society of Washington and the plans he had started to form for his future. As the train slowly pulled west, he felt nothing but the desperate need to get home as fast as he could.

On the long, hot trip back home, Talbot didn't let himself get too sentimental. Even if memories tried to creep in, he pushed them away. This wasn't the time to think about the past — an old friend was dying, the most loyal and understanding friend he had ever had. He realized just how much he had leaned on her over the years, and how lonely life would be without her. Over and over, he thought about her strong and gentle presence. More than once, he had to brush away tears, thinking that he would never again find comfort in her company or help ease her loneliness. But even with all this sadness, nothing prepared him for what he would see at Los Olivos.

He arrived late at night. Padre Ortega was away, so the only news he could get was that the Señora was still alive. He quickly sent a note saying he would visit her at eleven the next morning.

The next day, he rode through the hot, dry hills again, just a few weeks before his birthday. As he passed through the shady oaks near the house, he spotted a hammock hanging across the front porch. A woman was lying in it — he could see a thick black braid hanging down.

"That can't be the Señora," he thought. "Lying in a hammock?" Then it hit him — her illness must have taken away all her strength and weight.

His hands shook as he climbed off his horse and tied it to a tree. He stood there a moment, trying to steady himself, because he felt pale and shaken. But he had spent a lifetime learning self-control. In a few moments, he pulled himself together and walked up the steps toward the porch. Still, when he reached the hammock, he needed all his strength to stay standing.

The Señora was gone. Lying there was Delfina Carillo. Not the proud, shining beauty he remembered — her face was thin now, and little blue veins showed under her skin. But her features had become delicate and fine again. The heavy brown color that age and sorrow had brought was gone. Her skin was pale, her cheeks flushed with bright color. Her huge eyes looked even larger now, and her mouth, though a little drooped, had its lovely shape back. She wore a soft white robe trimmed with lace, and despite her weakness, she looked young again — about twenty-six — and she was beautiful.

"Delfina!" he whispered. "Delfina!" Then he sank into a chair, trembling, feeling the blood rush to his head. First there was the overwhelming shock and joy of seeing her like this — then a deep, sudden sadness hit him too. He missed the Señora, the strong and comforting friend she had been. He looked around, half-expecting to see her, but she was gone. Even Delfina's spirit seemed to have traveled back to her younger self.

Delfina looked at him for a moment before letting out a soft sigh. "Ah — it's Juan," she said.

She sat up quickly. "Listen," she said, speaking fast. "At first, I didn't know you — my mind was confused. Marcia told me later I kept thinking I was still a young girl. Even when my head is clear, I feel that way. I'm all alone, nothing around me to remind me I've aged — and I like it. When I first got sick, Herminia came to see me, but I wrote and told her to go ahead to Mexico. Later, when I got worse, I was glad the girls were gone. I was free to dream — dreams that made me happy. I relived the days when I was young and beautiful and everyone adored me. I'm glad I get to die with those memories instead of growing old and bitter like so many others."

She paused, breathing hard, but didn't lie back down. After a moment, she kept going:

"And many times, Juan, I thought of you. Strange, isn't it? Back then, I loved Enrique. But now, when I dream, I see you. I missed you so much. I read about you in the newspapers while you were away in Washington. Enrique's been gone for a long time now — and honestly, even before he died, the love that made me marry him had faded. I stayed loyal; I did my duty. But when I remember my youth, it's you I think of more."

She stopped again, her voice dropping lower.

"I always wondered why I didn't love you back then. You're such a fine man now. But in those days, I was dazzled by the caballeros — their fancy looks and smooth words. I didn't understand anything deeper. Looking back, I realize something important was missing in my life. I often sighed without knowing why. Now I know — if I could be young again, I would marry you. I would have been truly happy. But I was never really alive, Juan — not the way I could have been."

She fell back into the hammock, breathing unevenly. She pointed to a bottle of angelica wine on a small table, and John rushed to help her. He lifted her gently and held the glass to her lips. Slowly, some color returned to her face. She reached up and crossed her arms around his neck.

"Juan," she whispered, her voice soft and pleading, "you once loved me — I know you did. Sometimes I cried, thinking of how I hurt you. Pretend I'm young again. Love me like you did then. I don't have long... and it would make me so happy."

"It's easy to imagine," he said. "So easy. God knows it will be painful... but if I had known this day would come during all those hard years, I would have wished for it with all my heart."

The End

Thank You for Reading

Dear Reader,

We hope this timeless classic has sparked your imagination and enriched your literary journey. Now that you've turned the final page, we want to share a vision for the future of reading—one where every classic you've ever wanted to explore is at your fingertips, in a format that best suits your life.

We'd like to invite you to gain immediate, unlimited digital & audiobook access to hundreds of the most treasured literary classics ever written—along with the option to secure deluxe paperback, hardcover & box set editions at printing cost. Together, we can spark a new global literary renaissance alongside our small, independent publishing house called "The Library of Alexandria."

Thousands of years ago, the Library of Alexandria stood as a beacon of knowledge—until it was lost to history. We aim to reignite that spirit of preservation and discovery right now, in the modern age—only this time, it's accessible to all, in every language and every format.

Picture a world where every timeless classic, novel, poem, or philosophical treatise is not only available to read but also updated for today's readers—modernized, translated into any language or dialect, and ready to enjoy in any format you choose, whether that is in an eBook, audiobook, paperback, or deluxe hardcover & box set version a printing cost.

By joining our movement to rebuild the modern Library of Alexandria, you become part of an unprecedented mission to offer:

- **Unlimited Audiobook & eBook Access** to the Greatest Classics of All Time

  Instantly explore thousands of legendary works, from Plato and Shakespeare to Jane Austen and Leo Tolstoy. All are instantly ready to read or listen to, giving you a complete literary universe at your fingertips.

- **Paperback & Deluxe Editions at Printing Costs:**

  Purchase any title in a paperback, deluxe hardbound, or deluxe boxset edition at printing costs, shipped right to your doorstep. Curate your personal library of Alexandria with editions worthy of display—crafted to last, designed to captivate, and delivered straight to your door.

- **Modern translations for Contemporary Readers** in all languages and dialects

  Discover a vast selection of classics reimagined in clear, current language—no more struggling with outdated phrases or obscure references. Next to the original versions, we aim to offer translations in as many languages and dialects as possible.

  As we continue our translation efforts and add new languages, readers everywhere can connect with these works as if they were written today. By bridging linguistic divides, you're contributing to ensuring that these timeless stories become more meaningful, accessible, and inspiring for people across the globe.

- **Your Personal Library of Alexandria:**

  Over the months and years, you'll curate a unique physical archive of classics—each volume a testament to your taste, curiosity, and love of knowledge. It's not just about owning books—it's about curating a cultural legacy you'll cherish and pass down for generations to come.

- **Join a Global Literary Renaissance:**

  Your support fuels an ongoing mission: allowing us to reinvest in offering deluxe print editions (including special boxsets) at their true cost, broaden the range of available formats and translations, and extend the reach of these works to new audiences worldwide. By joining today, you're not just preserving a legacy of masterpieces; you set in motion a powerful wave of literary accessibility.

  We are more than a publisher—we're a movement, and we can't do it alone. Your support lets us scale our mission, preserving and reimagining history's greatest works for tomorrow's readers.

Become a Torchbearer of knowledge.

Thank you for picking up this book and allowing us into your literary journey. As you turn the pages, know that you're part of something larger: a global effort to keep these stories alive, share their wisdom across borders and generations, and spark a true cultural revival for the modern era.

If this resonates with you—please consider taking the next step by visiting:

www.libraryofalexandria.com

With gratitude and a shared love of knowledge,

The Modern Library of Alexandria Team

Visit:

www.libraryofalexandria.com

Or scan the code below:

www.ingramcontent.com/pod-product-compliance
Lightning Source LLC
Chambersburg PA
CBHW011354010726
47494CB00008B/2318